Kindness of a Stranger

by Scott A. Ferguson, Sr.

SUTTON, ALASKA

Relevant Publishers LLC
P.O. Box 505
Sutton, AK 99674

www.relevantpublishers.com

Publisher's Cataloging-In-Publication Data

Names: Ferguson, Sr., Scott A., author.
Title: Kindness of a Stranger / written by Scott A. Ferguson Sr.

Identifiers: LCCN: 2023943390 | ISBN 978-1953263155 (paperback) | ISBN 978-1953263162 (ebook)

Printed in the United States of America

DEDICATION

I would like to dedicate this book to my readers for their continued support that allows me to follow my dreams of being an author.

ACKNOWLEDGMENTS

As I write more and more books, Eileen Ennis Fox, together with Vickie Pessagno, continue to help mold them. It is only through their efforts that these stories become cohesive enough to present to a publisher. Once again, I would like to express my gratitude to them for all they do.

Table of Contents

PROLOGUE

It was well after three AM when the Camaro pulled up the driveway with its lights off. Kathleen leaned over and gave the boy a kiss....and another one...and another one. Thirty minutes later the front door finally opened and she snuck into the house. Or, so she thought.

As she closed the door, the hall light flashed on, and her heart jumped into her throat. She turned around. Standing by the library door, she saw her father. The deep frown on his face told her wasn't happy. But, then again, she couldn't remember the last time he looked happy. Straightening her clothes, her heart sank as she forced a smile and said, "Hi Daddy."

"Do you know what time it is?" he asked. Without waiting for an answer he continued, "It's almost four in the morning! What time is that to be coming in from a movie? Where have you been?"

"Well," she began, not knowing what to say. "We were talking and..."

"Talking? Is that what kids call it these days, talking?" he bellowed. "Kathleen, don't lie to me, I know you were probably in some dark alley doing things you have no business doing with a boy you're obviously too embarrassed by to introduce to your mother and me!"

She knew she would regret it, but she couldn't help herself. "I'm not embarrassed by Kevin, I'm embarrassed by you! Every time I bring a boy home, you subject him to the third degree! By the time we finally get out of here, he's so intimidated he never asks me out again. And if he does, you freak him out so much that he's afraid to even hold my hand!"

"I don't do that," he retorted. "I've always been polite and friendly to every boy you've brought home! Don't blame me for your miserable social life!"

She gave a sarcastic sort of bark, "It's not my social life that's miserable. It's my home life! Having to put up with you and your stupid archaic rules is ruining my social life! Admit it, if you had your way, I'd never leave this house except under armed guard and in a chastity belt! I'm sixteen, Daddy, not six! It's time you start treating like an adult and not a little child!"

Now it was his turn to laugh. "I treat you exactly as you deserve! If you ever came close to acting like an adult, I'd treat you more like one. But you don't. Instead, you act like the world should bow down at your feet because you're Kathleen Madison. Well, I've got news for you sweetheart, the rest of us are not impressed. You act like a spoiled little rich girl who thinks the world is her play toy!

"Now get your butt up to your room and stay there until I decide what your punishment will be!"

She glared at her father for a minute unblinking, and he glared right back. Suddenly, she stomped her foot, "Humph!" Then Kathleen stormed up the elaborate staircase toward her opulent bedroom. When she walked into her room, she turned, screaming, "I hate you!!" The force of the slamming door shook the frame.

He sighed and climbed the staircase to the master suite. His wife looked at him, her brows drawn together. "That didn't go well, did it? Next time, I think you should let me deal with her. It might be less explosive."

As he climbed into bed he replied, "Carolyn, I've had it. I'm done taking her lip and coddling her. She's grounded for at least the next month!"

Carolyn didn't respond. Instead, she leaned over and turned out the light.

Down the hall, their only daughter climbed silently out of her bedroom window and disappeared into the night.

CHAPTER 1

Life sure changed in the last six months, and not for the better. Looking back, Mike Hatfield didn't understand what had gone so wrong that he ended up living in a cheap motel, paid for by someone else, and contemplating his life.

The TV was on some stupid sporting event but he wasn't paying it any attention. On the bedside table, there was a half empty bottle of the cheapest whiskey he could find and a bottle of generic sleeping pills he'd been given at the free clinic.

Thirty-nine years old and nothing to show for it, he thought to himself. *No wife, no kids, no job and no future. What was left? Not a damned thing. He might as well do it. Nobody would miss him and nobody would give a damn.*

His wife, if he could still call her that, would probably be happy he was gone. At least she'd get the insurance money, that's more than he'd given her in the last six months. It was probably more than he could give her in the future too. As for his kids, they wouldn't miss him. Hell, they never tried to call him now while he was still alive. All in all, Mike figured, the world would be a whole lot better without him.

He decided to do it. He refilled his whiskey glass and picked up the sleeping pills. *How many should he take*, he wondered?

"What the hell," he mused, "Why not take them all? Might as well do it right." He twisted the cap off and upended the bottle of the pills into his shaking hand. For some unknown reason, he paused, staring at the pills for a few seconds. Taking a deep breath, he popped the pills into his mouth and washed them down with the whole tumbler full of whiskey.

Then, Mike lay back on the bed, waiting for them to take effect. *Should he have left a note telling the world how shitty he thought it was? Why bother, no one would read it anyway.* He began to feel sleepy and closed his eyes. Just before unconsciousness took him he thought, *God forgive me*, and was gone.

He didn't know where he was, but it sure was beautiful. Sunshine filtered through the leaves of the trees and a slight breeze brushed his cheek. The air was warm and scented with flowers. The grass was so thick and green, it looked like a velvet carpet. He began walking, looking at everything around him with astonishment and wide eyes. This place was calming, almost blissful. Thinking back, Mike couldn't remember being in a place like this before in his life.

As he was meandering through the lawn, he saw a man in the distance walking toward him. Something about the man looked vaguely familiar, but he couldn't put his finger on what it was. He found himself walking toward the man intentionally but didn't know why. Suddenly, he realized who the man was.

As Mike approached, the man smiled at him and called him by name. His grandfather appeared a lot younger than he'd ever seen him in real life. The reunion was all very strange but exciting. When they came together, they embraced. The hug lasted a long time. "Grandpa, it's so good to see you again!" Mike said as they hugged.

"It's good to see you too. I've waited so long for this day," he replied.

"Where are we?" he asked as they broke apart.

His grandfather didn't reply. Instead, he gestured forward with his hand, "Come and everything will be explained."

They began walking up a hill, towards what looked like a covered picnic pavilion. As Mike looked, he saw a lot of people under the pavilion. As they got nearer, he began to recognize most of them. Before him stood countless friends and relatives who had died. One by one, the people turned and recognized him. They smiled and called out. At last, he saw the one person above all he wanted to see. He saw his mother.

She took a step toward him, and he took a hurried step toward her. He picked up his pace as he neared her, eventually breaking into a run. As he came closer, he saw tears in her eyes. She could see tears in his eyes too. When they reached each other, their embrace was closer and longer than the one he shared with his grandfather. They looked into each other's eyes and found there was no need to say anything. Their hearts understood the unsaid words.

Others began gathering around him, smiling, shaking hands and slapping his back. The reunion seemed to last a long time. Eventually, after greeting everyone, his grandfather said, "Come with me, there's someone I'd like you to meet. He's been so looking forward to seeing you."

They began walking towards a man in an off-white robe. From behind, Mike could see the man had long dark brown hair and wore sandals. When they were a few feet away, the man turned around. Mike couldn't believe his eyes!

Immediately, without thinking, he fell to his knees. Mike dared not look up, staring at the man's feet. Unconsciously, Mike found himself reaching out for the hem of the man's robe. Hesitantly, he touched it.

Tears began to roll down his cheeks as he brought the garment to his face. In his mind's eye, Mike saw every mean and cruel thing he had ever done. He remembered every unkind act and thought he ever experienced. He also remembered what he had done at the end of his life. Regret and heartbreak consumed him.

The man reached down and touched him on the shoulder. With a gentle smile he spoke, "Rise and walk with me."

Immediately, the sadness left Mike as he looked up into the loving face smiling down at him. Rising to his feet, the man placed one arm around Mike's shoulder. They began to walk out from under the pavilion. The man encouraged, "I know what you're feeling, and there's no need. Even though you made mistakes, you've done well. All men have regrets, and you're no different. Still, I'm proud of you and well pleased so far. But you're not done. You don't belong here, yet."

Mike didn't understand. "I don't belong?" he asked. A sinking feeling filled his heart. He wanted to stay in this man's presence for the rest of his life. He wanted to stay here in this special place with all the people he loved and missed for so long.

The man smiled gently again, "No my son, you are not done. You've got to go back. There is still work for you to do. The next time you come here, you may stay. But for now, you must go back."

Mike could feel his heart breaking. He couldn't leave this man's presence! How could he go back to his old life when his heart would always be here, with this man? It wasn't fair. "But, I don't want to go back. I want to stay with you!" he blurted out.

He blushed as the man replied, "It is not your time."

"What do I have to do?" he asked.

"You'll know when the time comes. For now, it's enough for you to know that you must go back."

Mike looked behind them and saw the far away pavilion. It seemed as if it and the surrounding park was a shining island encompassed by vast darkness. The man was still talking, but his voice seemed far away, as if it were fading. "Keep your faith. All will be well. Now, my son, go in peace."

Mike opened his eyes and saw he was back in the dingy motel room. The drained whiskey bottle and empty bottle of sleeping pills were still on the bedside table. He was once again back in his miserable life, facing an empty future and an even emptier past. He wept bitterly.

As he cried, he remembered the man's words, *"There is still work for you to do."* What had he meant, work to do? Mike didn't have a job and there was very little likelihood of him finding one anytime soon. All he possessed was an old junker in the parking lot and about fifty dollars in his wallet.

His wife had taken the children when she went to her parent's house, their house having been repossessed after he'd lost his job. From where he laid, everything good that had ever happened to him never lasted long nor amounted to much. Still, the man said he had work to do. Mike got up, went to the bathroom, and washed his face with cold water. The chill woke him. When he looked in the mirror, he saw a man with just a glimmer of hope in his eyes. *Where did that come from?*

Mike walked out of the dark, dingy motel room and into a bright sunny morning. The cool air felt crisp as he took a deep breath. This was a new beginning for his life. Mike didn't know what he was supposed to do, but he felt ready. Today, he could do anything.

Getting in his car, he drove down the street to the little restaurant where he'd eaten dinner the night before. As he parked in front row of the parking lot, he saw a young woman, a kid really, standing looking through the window at the people and the food. Mike looked at her reflection in the glass and could see the hunger burning in her eyes. He wasn't sure if it was hunger for the food or the company of people. Either way, he felt he had to do something to help her.

She could see the man walking up behind her from the reflection in the window. His clothes looked as if he'd slept in them for days, his face unshaven. At first, she felt he meant her no good, but then she looked into his eyes. They seemed kind and benevolent. She could detect no malice in his eyes. Suddenly, she felt as if they were the eyes of a friend. Still, when he stopped beside her, weary she drew her arms around her.

"The food looks good, doesn't it?" he asked, not looking at her.

She didn't answer.

"I don't know about you, but I'm hungry. And a little company for breakfast would make it even better. Are you hungry?"

She could feel her stomach churn, gnawing at her. It had been three days since she'd eaten anything that could be called a meal. She'd had a few scraps dug out of the trash beside a fast food joint. Cold French fries and remnants of stale hamburger buns with bits of meat washed down by watered down sodas. She didn't even get to finish what she'd found before she was chased away by one of the burger joint's workers.

Yes, she was hungry. Yes, she would love some human company, but could she trust him? Somehow, deep inside, she felt she could. Yet, she couldn't help but wonder, *What did he want from her in exchange? But, what could he do to her in a restaurant full of people in the middle of the morning?*

After weighing all her options, at last she finally spoke, "Yes, I am."

"Well then, would you like to join me for some breakfast? I promise not to bite," he joked with a smile.

She nodded in agreement.

The pair entered the doors and sat in a booth near the front. Music from an old jukebox played an ancient song she'd never heard before. The waitress spotted them and came over, handing them each a menu. Mike ordered coffee and the girl ordered a hot chocolate. Once the waitress left, the young woman looked over the menu. Everything looked so delicious she couldn't decide what to order.

The man said, "I don't know about you, but I feel like some eggs, sausage and fried potatoes this morning. Maybe I'll even get an extra order of sausage. What looks good to you?"

Before she could stop herself she blurted out, "Everything! I haven't eaten a decent meal in days!" She stopped herself and blushed crimson. Finally after a few moments, she looked up.

Concern filled his brown eyes. It was the last thing she expected to see.

At last he asked, "Why not?'

She found herself wanting, almost needing to tell this man everything. Then alarm bells sounded in her head. She realized the truth would only get her in trouble. So, she decided to tell him her cover story.

"I just turned eighteen last month when I left home. I couldn't take listening to my mother and her boyfriend yelling and screaming at each other. The night before I left, it was worse than ever. They were both drunk when the usual argument broke out. Mom got so pissed off she picked up her glass and threw it at him. But she missed. He retaliated by grabbing her and hitting her upside the head.

"I couldn't just stand by and watch my mother get beaten up so I grabbed a bat and hit him. I must not have hit him hard enough, because he stopped beating on her and went for me. He grabbed me by the hair and began hitting me instead. Mom finally stopped him. She picked up the bat and bashed him on the back of the head. He let go of me and dropped in a heap to the floor. Then, Mom just kept hitting him. Over and over she hit him. Finally, I came to my senses enough to stop her. I put her to bed and called the police. When they arrived, they took her boyfriend to the hospital and arrested my mom. I tried to stop them, but the police said there was nothing they could do. In domestic violence cases, someone had to go to jail. So, they carted her off and I left. I wound up here, walking the streets with nowhere to go."

As their food came, Mike stated, "You're lucky you haven't been hurt walking the streets alone. Aren't you scared someone might attack you?"

In between mouthfuls she answered, "Yeah. I've been scared out of my mind, but... I guess I've been lucky. Nobody's even given me a second look. That is, until today, when I met you."

They sat in silence, eating their breakfast, each lost in their own thoughts. Finally, she asked, "So, what's your story?"

He wiped his mouth and took a sip of coffee before answering, "Well, I'm thirty-nine. Until recently, I was married with two teenage children. Now, I'm an unemployed middle-age man with no one who gives a damn about him, no job and no future."

A look of concerned flashed across her face. "What happened?"

"The company I worked for went belly up, and I was out of a job. We went from living on a comfortable salary to living off of unemployment and eventually food stamps. I kept looking for work, but I couldn't find another job. Meanwhile, the bills kept piling up, and my wife couldn't deal with it any more.

"I think the final straw was when the mortgage company foreclosed on the house. We had nowhere to go. She took the kids and moved back to her parent's house without me. She says I'm not the man she married anymore and until I am, she doesn't want to see me again.

"That was a month ago. Since then, I've been living in a sleazebag motel feeling sorry for myself. I even had to pawn my wedding ring to pay for food. I keep looking for a job, but no one wants to hire a used-up middle-age man with few skills and even less potential."

When Mike finished his story, the woman looked up and said, "I guess that makes us a couple of losers."

"Yeah, I guess it does."

They finished their breakfast and walked out of the restaurant. Walking by his car, he stopped. The young lady looked at him and said, "Well, thanks for breakfast. I guess I'll be going now."

As she started to walk away he called out, "Wait! Where are you going to go?"

"I don't know. I guess I'll just walk around for a while and see what comes up."

He looked slightly embarrassed as he offered, "If you want, you can come back to my room."

She eyed him suspiciously.

Suddenly, he realized how that sounded and what she must be thinking. Blushing, he stammered, "I didn't mean it that way. Oh my God, what you must be thinking of me! I'm sorry; that came out all wrong. What I meant was, I've got a couple of job interviews today so I won't be there. If you want, you could clean up a little and maybe watch TV or take a nap. Then, maybe, when I got back, we could eat dinner."

She continued staring at him.

He continued blushing and stammering.

Finally, she asked, "Why are you being so nice to me? You don't know me. What am I to you?"

He thought about that for a moment. "I don't know," he finally stated. "I need a friend I guess, and you look like you need one too." She seemed to be thinking about that when he continued, "I guess that sounds a little weird," he admitted. "But I didn't mean it in any negative way."

She gave him a tentative smile, "Don't worry about it. I know you didn't mean it that way. But, I don't think it's a good idea. Anyway, I've got something else to do too. Thanks again for breakfast."

They stood, looking awkwardly at each other for a few seconds, then she said, "Well, I'd better be going."

The girl turned and began walking away. When she was a few steps away, he called to her. "Wait a minute!" He jogged a few yards and stood in front of her. Reaching into his shirt pocket, he took out a piece of paper and a pen. He quickly wrote on the paper then handed it to her.

"Take this." As she looked down at the paper, he continued, "It's my name and the address and phone number of the motel I'm staying at." After an awkward pause he said, "In case you need anything."

Reluctantly, she nodded her head, "Thanks."

As she turned to go, he cried out again, "Wait!" When she turned around, he stated, "You haven't told me your name."

"My name is Kitty. Kitty Benson." Then, she walked away.

CHAPTER 2

Mike went back to his room, cleaned up, and drove to his first appointment. As usual, the interview went poorly. At the end, the interviewer thanked him for his time and said they would get back to him once they made a final decision. Mike knew he wouldn't be hearing from them anytime soon.

After a cheap and tasteless lunch, he went to his second interview. This time the interview went well. It seemed to him every question was written with his resume in mind. He felt he had all the right answers. At the conclusion, the interviewer said, "I think that's about all the questions I have. When can you start?"

Mike tried to suppress a grin but couldn't quite do it. "I can start tomorrow or any day that's good for you."

"Excellent," replied the interviewer, "Is tomorrow okay?"

He nodded.

"Good, report to Human Resources tomorrow at nine AM." The interviewer stood up and offered him her hand. He gladly shook it as she said, "Congratulations, Mr. Hatfield. Welcome aboard. I look forward to working with you."

That night, Mike called his wife to tell her the good news. Her response was, "Good, now you can help support your kids and my parents won't have to foot all the bills."

That wasn't the answer he was hoping for. "Aren't you coming back," he asked.

She laughed mirthlessly. "I spent almost twenty years with you and what do I have to show for it? Nothing. No, I think I'll cut my losses and start over."

There was dead silence on his end of the line.

She went on, "I'm sorry, Mike, I just don't think we have a future together anymore."

He couldn't respond. His insides felt hollow, as if they were completely gone. What could he say? There were no words in the English language to express how he felt. Yet, he had to say something. Finally, he said, "You don't mean that."

"Yes, Mike, I think I do." After a long pause she said, "I don't know, maybe after you get back on your feet... And I've had time to think it over... I might change my mind. But, for the time being, I do mean it."

Once again, there was silence on the line.

At last she spoke, "Take care of yourself, Mike."

Then he heard a click as she hung up the phone.

He put the receiver back onto its cradle and stared at the phone. His whole world, everything he believed in and wanted in life, was gone. *What's the use,* he asked himself. He didn't have an answer. Instead, he lay down on the bed and curled into a ball. Then the tears came. His body shook with sobs as he tried to cry out his grief and misery into the pillow. It seemed he wept for hours, but no matter how much or how hard he cried, it didn't relieve the pain.

When Kitty walked away from the breakfast man, she wasn't sure where she was going. As she wandered, she thought how strange that guy had been. She wasn't sure if he was creepy or just a lonely old guy. Either way, she wasn't the kind of girl to go to some strange guy's hotel room and take her chances he was a nice guy. She may be broke with no place to go, but she wasn't that desperate. And certainly not that trusting. Still, his eyes haunted her memory. They made her feel she could trust him.

She walked aimlessly around town for hours. Sometime in the afternoon, she found herself in a park near a playground. She watched the children playing. Their mothers kept an eye on them, gossiping among themselves on the benches nearby. It brought back memories Kitty didn't want to face. She remembered going to a playground when she was a little, but, in her case, there was no mother to watch over her, only a nanny. Try as she might, Kitty couldn't recall her mother doing anything with her. In fact, she couldn't remember either of her parents paying any attention to her at all.

She walked away feeling even more lonely than when she'd stopped to watch. She continued to amble through the park, not really paying attention to where she was going or what she was seeing. When the sun started going down, Kitty felt the cool night air against her skin and a familiar gnawing in her stomach. She guessed it was time to figure out where she was going to get her next meal and where to spend this cold and dreary night.

She wandered into downtown where she saw people and families walking and talking. Couples held hands and chatted happily to each other about the day. Everyone seemed to be enjoying each other's company on their way home from work. She looked away. Further on, she noticed families coming out of a movie theater laughing as they discussed the movie. She saw parents holding their children's hands and occasionally carrying a sleeping child over their shoulder. A reminder of just one more thing she couldn't remember her parents doing.

As the night drew on, it became colder and darker. She shivered as she turned a corner. A group of guys stood outside a bar, smoking cigarettes. She thought about turning around to avoid them, but decided it would be best to keep moving forward and go around them. As she approached, one of them called out, "Hey baby, you sure look good!"

The others laughed.

Kitty tried to appear as if she didn't hear him and began walking a little faster. She had a bad feeling about this guy and wanted to get away from him as soon as she could.

Almost parallel to him now, the man egged on by his buddies, tried again, "What I could do with a chick like that, mmm, mmm, mmm. What do ya say? Wanna have some fun tonight?"

She kept her head down as she walked past. She hoped she could walk away without anything else being said. Too bad it didn't work out that way.

After she past the group of men, she felt her guard relax a little, thinking she was safe enough away they'd soon forget her. Suddenly, the big mouthed guy grabbed her arm from behind.

Jerking her arm, she tried to pull it out of his grip. His buddies laughed as she said, "Let me go!"

His grip tightened on her arm. When it started to hurt, he asked,

"What's the matter, too good for me?"

She continued to struggle. "Let me go!" she cried even louder. Kitty hoped if she caused a scene, someone would help her. Unfortunately, that didn't work either.

"Bitch, I asked you a question," the man growled, pulling her towards him.

One of his friends chimed in taunting, "I don't think she likes you, Al. Maybe you're not her type."

The others laughed, but not Al. The alcohol they'd consumed now made him suddenly angry. "Not her type, eh? I'll show her what her type is."

Al pulled Kitty into a nearby alley. As she struggled to get away, the others laughed even louder. With her free hand, Kitty reached out and slapped Al across the face. She continued screaming, "Let me go!" and "Help, somebody please help me!"

Al felt the sting of her slap. It made him even madder than ever. Doubling up his fist, he pulled it back and punched her in the mouth.

Kitty tasted blood and could feel at least two loose teeth in her jaw. She spat the blood out on the asphalt. She screamed again for help at the top of her lungs. Again, Al hit her.

Her head was spinning as Al yelled, "I'll teach you... You little bitch!"

Kitty tried to cover her head with her free arm, but Al's hard fists kept hitting her anywhere he could. Blow after blow reigned down on her body, striking her seemingly everywhere. When she could barely stand, he reached out and grabbed the front of her shirt and pulled.

The fabric ripped away, exposing her bra. The sight of it seemed to send Al into a sexual frenzy. Redoubling her efforts to defend herself, Kitty swung her hand out and raked Al's face with her fingernails, causing four deep gouges in his cheek. He let out a scream of pain and momentarily let go of her arm. She took two steps in a run before he grabbed her by her hair and swung her around. Then, he slammed her face into a brick wall.

That was the last Kitty remembered.

Two hours later, Al and his buddies left the alley and went home to their wives and girlfriends. An hour after that, a police cruiser found Kitty's body, unconscious in the alley.

Mike woke to the sound of someone pounding on the door of his room. Groggily, he got up, threw his pants on, and opened the door. Two police officers stood in front of him along with a man in a suit. One officer shined a flashlight into his room, looking for heaven knows what. The other officer stood by as the man in the suit, "Are you Mike Hatfield?"

Mike scratched his head, "Yeah, that's me. Why? Is there something wrong officer?"

The man asked, "Do you know a Kathleen Benson?"

Mike racked his brain. *What is this guy talking about?* He'd never heard of anyone named Kathleen Benson. Then, a light went on. From somewhere in the back of his mind, he recalled the girl he invited to breakfast. *What did she say her name was? Wasn't it something Benson? Kate or Cat or, wait a minute, that was it; Kitty! Kitty Benson!*

He looked at the man and slowly nodded. "I think I might," he answered slowly. "Only, she told me her name was Kitty, not Kathleen."

The man didn't respond. "Are you a relative of the girl?"

"No," Mike answered, "Just a friend. I met her this morning, yesterday morning I mean. We had breakfast together. Why, what's happened?"

"Mr. Hatfield, could you come with us please? We have a few questions we'd like you to answer."

Mike was getting irritated now, "No, I will not go with you. Not until I get some answers. Why are you asking all these questions? What's happened?"

The man consulted his notebook. "At about one AM this morning, we found Kathleen in an alley off Washington Street. She'd been beaten and assaulted. She's in City General Hospital in Intensive Care. The only thing we found at the crime scene was her identification card and a piece of paper with your name, a phone number, and this motel room on it in her pocket."

Mike's jaw dropped. "Oh, my God," he whispered, remembering he'd given her his information just in case she needed help. "Who did it?" he asked. "Did you catch the bastard?"

"That's what we want to talk to you about," he replied. "Please come with us, Sir."

"Okay, fine," he agreed. "Just let me get my keys, and I'll follow you."

As he turned to go back into the room, the man in the suit said, "That won't be necessary, Sir. You can ride with me." He stood back and motioned to a plain, nondescript sedan.

Mike was stunned. "Am I under arrest or something?"

"No, Sir. Can we go now, please?"

Mike grabbed the room key and a shirt, "Yeah, sure. Let's go."

They walked to the car and Mike got in the passenger's seat. As the man pulled left out of the motel's parking lot, he said, "I haven't introduced myself. I'm Detective Marcus Cooper."

Mike, still deep in his own thoughts and miseries, mumbled, "Nice to meet you, Detective." After a moment he said, "Where are we going?"

Detective Cooper ignored the question and asked, "How long have you known Ms. Benson?"

Mike replied, "Like I said, I just met her this morning. I bought her breakfast, and we talked for a while."

"Did she tell you anything about where she came from? Anything about her relatives; anyone we can contact?"

"No, well, yes, I guess. She said she left home because her mother and her mother's boyfriend were always drunk and fighting. Finally, they came to blows and she got in the middle of it. Her mother ended up getting arrested and she ran away. That's really all I know."

Detective Cooper was silent for a few seconds, processing the information Mike had just given him. Finally, he asked, "When you parted company, did she give you any indication where she was going to go or what she was going to do that day?"

Mike thought for a moment before responding, "No, she didn't say. Well, that's not entirely true. She said she had something to do, but she didn't say what it was. I didn't believe her. She gave me the impression she didn't really have anything to do and no place to go."

The unmarked police car pulled into the hospital parking lot and Detective Cooper continued, "Well, that's not much but it's something." He pulled into a parking spot, "Come on, we can go see her. If we're lucky, she might be awake."

In a few minutes, they were standing beside Kitty's bed in the intensive care unit. She was messed up, bad. Her face was a swollen mass of cuts and bruises. Tubes, IV lines, and monitors were attached to almost every part of her body. Mike couldn't believe this was the same girl he'd eaten breakfast with less than twenty-four hours ago.

"What's wrong with her?" he asked the detective.

Before the detective could answer, a nurse came in. She looked at both men, "I'm sorry, gentlemen, Ms. Benson isn't allowed any visitors."

Detective Cooper showed her his identification folder and asked, "Can you tell us what her injuries are?"

The nurse looked at the folder and answered, "She has several broken bones in her face and head, a broken jaw, several broken ribs, a severe concussion, ruptured spleen, bruised and lacerated kidneys, a dislocated shoulder, collapsed lung, possible spinal injuries and injuries to her reproductive organs."

"And, how's she doing?" the detective inquired further.

"She came through surgery alright, but we'll have to wait and see how she heals."

The nurse moved next to the bed and began typing on a computer tablet. When she was done she excused herself saying, "Her doctor should be here in a few minutes if you want to talk to him."

Detective Cooper said that wasn't necessary and thanked her for the information. Mike looked down at Kitty's face. He couldn't believe this beaten and bruised person could be the same pretty girl he'd invited for breakfast the day before. Without looking at him, Mike asked the detective, "How could someone do this to a poor young girl?"

The detective answered, "I don't know. I've been doing this for over fifteen years and never been able to understand why people do this kind of thing."

They left the hospital ten minutes later. On their way out, they stopped at the nurse's station where Detective Cooper told the staff Mike Hatfield would be authorized access to Kitty's room anytime.

Then Cooper drove Mike back to his motel room. Before Mike got out of the car, Cooper handed him his business card, "That's my office and cell number. You can reach me any time of the day or night. If you think of anything that might help us with the investigation don't hesitate to call."

Mike thanked him, and they shook hands before he stepped out of the car. Numbly, Mike watched as the detective drove away. Half an hour later, Mike was in his car on his way to his new job.

CHAPTER 3

For the next ten days, Mike would go to work in the morning and spend the evenings in Kitty's hospital room. For the life of him, he couldn't think why he was doing it. He liked the girl, but she was nothing to him. Yet, something was drawing him to her. It wasn't a romantic feeling, which would have been disgusting. No, it was more of a desire to take care of her, kind of like a father wants to take care of his children. Maybe he was transferring his feelings for his own kids onto her...maybe.

Late on the tenth night, Kitty started to stir. When she opened her eyes, Mike was the first thing she saw.

He smiled at her, "How are you feeling?"

She mumbled, "Not too good. Where am I? What are you doing here?"

"You're in City General Hospital. The night you were brought here, the police came knocking at my door. They brought me over and told me what happened to you. I've been here every evening since."

As he finished speaking, the nurse came in. As soon as she saw Kitty was awake, she pushed Mike out of the room and called the doctor. Within minutes, four doctors and five technicians crowded around her bed. Mike walked over to the nurse's desk and called Detective Cooper. Within another half hour, he was there too.

Mike followed the detective into Kitty's room. A young woman glowered at them as they entered. "Who are you, and what are you doing here?"

Detective Cooper introduced himself and Mike. He didn't say Mike was with the police, but he didn't say he wasn't either. *If she isn't going to ask,* he reasoned to himself, *I'm not going to elaborate.* Once the doctors finished their examination, Cooper stepped out of the room to get the results. They weren't good.

Mike went back to Kitty's bedside. He smiled as he looked down at her. She didn't smile back. Not that she didn't want to smile back, she did, but she couldn't. Her injuries didn't let her do much of anything with her face. "So, what did the doctors say," she asked through clenched teeth, since her jaw was wired shut.

Just then, Detective Cooper walked back through the door. He walked up to the opposite side of her bed, looked down at her. "Ms. Benson, I'm Detective Marcus Cooper from the Metropolitan Police. I'll be investigating your case. Do you feel up to telling me what you remember about the night you were attacked?"

Kitty thought back. *What did she remember about that night? It was all just a blur.* She stated, "Detective, right now I don't even remember my name. Let alone what happened to me. Can I think about it for a day or two and get back to you?"

"Of course you can. Mike's got my number. If you need anything, give me a call. In the meantime, please don't discuss the incident with anyone." At that point, he looked directly at Mike, "except the doctors, okay?"

She nodded.

Cooper left, and Kitty looked at Mike, tears flowing down her bandaged face. "Mike," she sobbed, "I can't feel my legs. I can't feel anything below my chest. I don't want to be paralyzed! What am I going to do?"

Mike took her hand in his. It felt warm but lifeless. He smiled at her, looking deep into her eyes, "We'll deal with it." The look in his eyes was warm and comforting. Yet, inside he was devastated for her. *What were they going to do?* He didn't have an answer.

Just then, the doctor came back in. She looked at Mike and asked, "Am I allowed to see my patient in private, or must you remain in here with us?"

Before he could answer, Kitty spoke, "He's my friend. Anything you have to say to me, you can say in front of him."

The doctor glared at both of them.

What was she thinking, Mike wondered? He found he really didn't care.

The doctor shrugged, "As you wish. Now to bring you up to speed, Ms. Benson, let me tell you about your injuries. As you can tell, your jaw is broken. So is you left cheek, several ribs, and your left collar bone. We had to remove your spleen and re-inflate one of your lungs. You also received lacerations and bruising to your kidneys, but they'll heal on their own. That was the easy part." The doctor took in a deep breath before continuing, "Now for the hard part, you suffered a severe concussion. We don't know what, if any damage it caused. You also suffered a spinal injury. That's why you can't feel anything below your chest at the moment. We did an MRI and didn't see any permanent damage, so the paralysis may only be temporary. We'll run some more tests to be sure."

The doctor looked uncomfortable as she paused to look at Mike again. She looked back at Kitty and continued, "Do you remember what happened to you?"

Kitty shook her head.

"It seems you were raped repeatedly," the doctor stated.

Kitty's eyes widened with terror.

The doctor continued, "This caused major damage to you reproductive system. I'm afraid we couldn't repair the damage and had to perform a hysterectomy... I'm sorry." With that, the doctor gave Mike another pitiful look and left the room.

Mike didn't know what to say. He was dumbfounded.

Kitty laid in her bed, tears streaming down her cheeks. Silence filled the room.

Mike moved over to the side of Kitty's bed. Taking a tissue, he began to wipe her tears. Her eyes had closed, but as soon as she felt the soft pressure on her face, her eyes flew open.

They stared at each other for a few moments. Mike could see the pain in her eyes, and she could see the guilt in his. Both sets of eyes brimmed with tears. Kitty took a shuddering breath, and in barely a whisper breathed, "Thank you."

Mike smiled kindly, "Kitty, I'm so sorry."

She asked, "What do you have to be sorry for? You didn't do this to me. I did it to myself. I shouldn't have left home. I shouldn't have been in that part of town." She turned her head to the side as the tears began to flow once again.

Mike felt helpless. He couldn't think of anything to say. There wasn't really anything he could do. Finally, Kitty turned back toward him and said, "Mike, I'm really sorry, but I think I'd like to be alone, if you don't mind."

Mike just nodded, slowly turned, and headed for the door. Once he was outside, he walked with a heavy heart back to his car. The drive home was silent, as he couldn't stop thinking. He never felt so bad for anyone in his life. *Well, that wasn't entirely true. There was one person who he had felt this bad for: himself.*

The next day, when Mike arrived at the hospital, the nurse told him Kitty gave orders that she didn't want to see anyone. Stunned, he left. He didn't understand. *What had he done that she wouldn't see him?*

For the rest of the week, Kitty refused to see Mike. The nurse, whose name was Sandy, felt sorry for him. She told him he shouldn't take it personally. Kitty refused to see anyone except the medical staff that she couldn't refuse.

Mike was determined not to let this turn of events get him down. He decided to use the time to find a place to live other than the motel. So, for the rest of the week, Mike stopped by the hospital to see Kitty. Each day he was turned away. So, he spent the evenings driving around, looking for an apartment. On the third day of his search, he finally found what he was looking for.

The apartment was small, only one bedroom, but it was clean and in a decent neighborhood. He signed the lease and moved in the next day. For the rest of the week, he continued to try to see Kitty. She continued to refuse to see him, so he spent the rest of the night making the apartment as comfortable as possible.

Kitty didn't want to see or talk to anyone. She didn't want to speak to the nurses or the doctors. She didn't want to see Detective Cooper, and she absolutely refused to see Mike. She couldn't move and didn't want to. All she wanted to do was die.

After about four days of deep despair, Kitty began to feel a tingling in her hands. At first this was exciting, but after hours of pins and needles in her hands, it began to get bothersome. By the second day, the sensation began to drive her nuts. The next time the attending physician came in, she told her about the sensation. The doctor smiled. It was the first good news she'd had in days. "I was hoping this would happen. It means the swelling in your spinal cord is subsiding. We'll do another MRI to see how well you're healing. Who knows, it might mean you'll be on your feet again someday."

After the MRI the doctor came back, accompanied by a man Kitty didn't know. "Kitty, this is Dr. Roth, he's a neurologist who specializes in trauma to the spinal cord," her doctor said.

Dr. Roth smiled and nodded. "I've looked at your MRI, and it looks good. There isn't much swelling left, but there does seem to be another problem. You have a ruptured disc in the thoracic region. That, in and of itself would not be too bad, except the disc ruptured into the spinal cord. This rupture is causing pressure on the cord and may be why you can't feel anything below your chest."

Kitty asked, "What about the tingling in my hands, it's driving me crazy."

Dr. Roth said, "As the swelling subsides, the sensation will decrease. Until then, there really isn't anything we can do for you. But I really came in to talk to you about the disc. Once the swelling recedes, I would like to go in and remove the bad disc. We would of course replace it with a mechanical one. Once completed, there is a good chance you'll regain feeling in your legs. To monitor the swelling, we'll be doing MRI's over the next few days. In the meantime, we'll need you to tell us if the sensations in you extremities change at all."

For the first time in weeks, Kitty felt a glimmer of hope growing in her heart. She actually smiled at the doctor as she asked, "Do you have any idea how long it will take for the swelling to go away?"

"No," the doctor replied, "there's really no way to tell. That's why we'll need to do periodic MRI's. Well, that's where we are. From now on, someone will be asking you about the sensations in your hands and whether or not you can feel anything below your chest." With that, the two doctors walked out.

Later that night, when Mike stopped by the hospital, the nurse was relieved to tell him Kitty would see him. When she gave him the good news on her progress, he felt excitement grow inside. He was happy for her.

"That's great!" he exclaimed. "If all goes well, you should be back on your feet in no time. I'm really happy for you, Kitty."

She asked him what had been going on with him while she was pouting; her words, not his. He told her about the new apartment and how the new job was going well. They talked for hours about everything under the sun.

It's good to have someone to talk to again, she thought to herself.

Mike found he had really missed talking to her too. He thought how lonely he felt when she wouldn't see him.

The next day when Mike went to see Kitty, he found she had been moved to another room. Nurse Sandy told him Kitty didn't need to be in Intensive Care anymore, so they moved her to the Orthopedic Floor. She gave him Kitty's new room number, and he left.

When he walked into the room, he saw Kitty sitting up in bed, watching TV. "I was hoping you'd find me," she greeted.

"When did they move you?"

"About 1:30 this afternoon, I think. It was funny. They took me for an MRI, and instead of bringing me back to ICU, they brought me here. It's a lot nicer. I have real walls instead of glass partitions. It gives me a little privacy."

"What did the doctor say about your test?" Mike asked.

Kitty's good mood seemed to deflate instantly, "There's no change. The swelling hasn't gone down any, and I still can't feel my legs."

"Well, there's always next time," Mike sounded encouraging.

Kitty suddenly brightened. "There is one piece of good news," she told him. She raised her hands and began flexing them. "Look, my arms and hands are starting to work again. I'm a little clumsy still, but they're getting better."

After about two hours of visiting, Mike headed back to his apartment.

The next day Mike was called in to his boss's office. As he walked in, he wondered what he'd done wrong. *Guilty conscience I guess,* he thought to himself. He tapped lightly on the door. When she looked up, Mike asked, "You wanted to see me?"

She smiled, "Yes, Mike. Come in please and have a seat."

As he sat down, she continued, "You've been with the company for a little over a month now. I thought it was time we had a little chat." Seeing the look on his face she quickly added, "Don't look so worried; you're not in trouble. I'm not going to fire you."

He relaxed and returned her smile.

"Actually, I think you're doing a great job. Since you've been here, production as gone up dramatically. I wish I had a dozen employees like you, Mike. And to show our appreciation for all your hard work, beginning next week, you'll be receiving a raise."

Mike's jaw dropped. He quickly closed it again, "I don't know what to say."

His boss laughed. "I think," she said jokingly, "That 'thank you' should just about cover it."

Mike blushed.

She laughed again.

"I'm sorry, I meant to say thanks. I don't know what else to say."

"You don't have to say anything. Just keep up the good work, Mike."

That evening, Mike felt like celebrating. He brought flowers and Kentucky Fried Chicken dinners when he arrived to see Kitty. What he saw when he entered her room ended his good mood.

Kitty was lying in her bed crying.

"What's wrong?" he asked.

Through her sobs, Kitty explained, "Dr. Roth came in and told me he doesn't believe the swelling is going to go down. I may never walk again!"

Mike was stunned. "Didn't he have any good news?"

"No. He said there was no reason to remove the ruptured disc if the swelling didn't go down. Mike, I don't want to spend the rest of my life in a wheelchair! What am I going to do?"

CHAPTER 4

"I guess we'll have to get a second opinion. Maybe another doctor will have a different diagnosis," Mike reassured.

Kitty didn't respond. She just laid there crying. Mike tried to cheer her up by giving her the flowers and offering her some chicken. But, it didn't help. She thanked him for the flowers, but didn't look at them. As for the chicken, she said she wasn't hungry. "Mike, would you mind going? I'd kind of like to be alone tonight."

Mike agreed. He put the flowers by her bedside and left the chicken dinner on the tray-table. As he walked out to the parking lot, he heard someone calling his name. Looking around and saw Sandy, the nurse from the ICU. "Hi, Sandy, how are you?"

As she walked toward him she smiled, "Oh, fine. How's Kitty doing? I haven't had a chance to stop in and see her."

"Not well, I'm afraid. One of her doctors told her he wouldn't do surgery to remove the ruptured disc in her back. He said it wasn't needed because the swelling in her spinal cord hasn't gone down."

"Which doctor was that?" Sandy asked.

"I think his name is Rose or something like that. Anyway, Kitty's pretty down about the whole thing."

"Dr. Roth? Simon Roth? He's useless. That sounds like something he would say. He's lazy and only does surgery if he can't get out of it."

"Yeah, well I told Kitty that she needed to get a second opinion. Maybe she can find a surgeon who will do the surgery even if she never walks again. You know, I'm not a doctor, but it seems to me that if the disc ruptured into the cord, it just might be causing the swelling, or at least, keeping the swelling from going down."

Sandy looked around, making sure no one was around. She opened her purse and took out a piece of paper and a pen. As she scribbled something on the paper, she leaned closer to Mike. In barely above a whisper, she spoke, "This is my home number. My husband is a neurosurgeon. He may be able to help. Once Kitty is released, have her call him." She looked up at Mike. "I'll tell him what I know about the case and tell him to expect the call."

Mike looked at the paper in his hand, "Thanks, Sandy. I'll give this to Kitty the next time I see her."

Sandy cautioned, "Don't give her the number until after she's out of the hospital. If anyone found out I gave it to you, it could cost me my job."

Mike assured her he wouldn't give it to Kitty until she was released. They talked for a few more minutes and then left the parking lot.

When Mike got home, he found he had a message on his answering machine. "Mike, it's Sharron. Give me a call when you get in. I have something I have to tell you."

He picked up the phone and dialed his wife's number.

She answered on the fourth ring.

"What's up?" he asked.

There was a long pause before she spoke, "I don't know how to tell you this, but I've met someone else." When Mike didn't say anything, she went on. "Mike, I'm really sorry. I didn't plan on meeting anyone, it just happened."

When he still didn't respond, Sharron continued, "I've contacted an attorney. I'm filing for divorce. He'll be sending you the papers in the next few days."

Mike was still silent.

She added, "I'm not asking for alimony or anything like that, just child support. I think that's fair, don't you?"

Mike was too dumbstruck to speak.

Sharron asked, "Mike, are you there?"

"Yes," he croaked, "I'm here."

"Well, say something. Yell at me. Scream at me. Do something!"

After a second, Mike answered, "Do the kids know?"

"Yes," she replied. "They've met him and seem to like him. My parents like him too."

Mike didn't say anything else. He simply hung up the phone. He walked slowly into the bedroom and lay down on the bed. For hours, he lay staring at the ceiling. Finally, he got up, got undressed, and crawled back into bed under the covers. He never shed a tear. When the sun came up, Mike was still laying on his back staring at the ceiling.

Kitty started physical therapy the day after Dr. Roth's verdict. The therapist was teaching her how to use a wheelchair. She learned how to get in and out of it, how to maneuver around, and generally become proficient. She wasn't really interested and didn't want to bother. Midway through the session, however, she discovered she was going to be discharged at the end of the week.

By the time Mike stopped by that evening, Kitty was depressed. "I found out today they're kicking me out at the end of the week. Mike, I don't have any place to go. Since I'm basically a charity case, I don't have any way to pay for a rehab facility or anything else. Mike, I don't know what I'm going to do!"

"You can live at my place. I've got room."

"We've had this conversation, Mike. I don't think that's a good idea."

"Kitty, where are you going to go, if you don't stay with me? You can't very well live on the streets in a wheelchair."

"But, I can't live with you either. What would your wife say? What would people think? A guy your age living with a crippled girl my age?"

"As far as my wife is concerned," Mike said in a flat voice, "you don't have to worry about that, she's divorcing me."

"Oh Mike! I'm so sorry. Is there anything I can do?"

"No, there's nothing anyone can do. I've just got to learn to live with it."

There was silence for a few moments.

Then, Kitty spoke again. "Detective Cooper stopped by to see me today. He told me the investigation was nearing a close. He thought he might be making a couple of arrests in a few days. He had me look at a bunch of pictures to see if I could identify my attackers. I picked out one guy I thought was one of them, but I wasn't sure."

"Did he say if your information was any help?"

"He said it was something to go on. Cooper said when he added that information to the physical evidence he had, he thought he had a pretty good case."

"What evidence?"

"When I was brought into the ER, they found skin and blood under my fingernails. And they took other samples too," Kitty blushed. "Cooper thinks they may be able to identify my attackers from the DNA evidence."

"Did he say when he was going to make the arrests?"

"No, he said it depends on how the interviews went. There is a chance he won't be able to arrest anyone. It all depends on the evidence and if they could get an identification from it. If they couldn't, then my case may never be closed."

"And that's another reason why you should move in with me. Look what happened the last time you tried to live on the streets. If Cooper doesn't get a break, those guys will still be on the loose. Who knows if they could track you down, and this time they might kill you."

Kitty was exasperated, "What is it with you? Exactly why do you want me to move in with you? It can't be sex. I'm damaged goods. I can't do anything else for you. I don't cook. I don't clean, and I don't have any money. What's in it for you?"

"Kitty, there's nothing in it for me. For some strange reason I can't explain, I kinda think of you as the daughter I never had... So sex would be disgusting. I care about you as a friend."

Kitty thought about it for a minute. Finally, she gave in. "Alright, if I can't find somewhere else to go, I'll stay with you for a while. But, only until I can get on my feet and take care of myself."

After a second, she began laughing, "What a bad joke, on my feet again!"

Mike began laughing too. They both laughed for a minute or two. It was good to laugh. They both needed to laugh, after all, neither of them had much to laugh about recently.

After the laughter died down, Mike said, "It's settled then, on Friday you'll move in with me."

The rest of the week was busy for both of them. Kitty worked hard on her therapy, and Mike made sure the apartment would be ready for her when she arrived. To this end, Mike went to the landlord and asked if he could add lift bars to the bathroom and make other minor alterations to accommodate Kitty's wheelchair. The landlord not only agreed but also offered to help pay for it.

On the morning of the second day after talking to his soon-to-be ex-wife, Mike was getting ready for work when there was a knock on the door. When he opened it, there was a messenger with an envelope. After signing for it, Mike went back to his kitchen and poured his first cup of coffee for the day. He looked at the envelope and saw it was from a lawyer in his wife's home town. As he opened it, he knew what was inside: the divorce papers his wife told him were coming. He put them back in the envelope and took them with him to the office.

Once he sat at his desk, he took out the envelope. He read the papers and realized he was going to need a lawyer to help him navigate through this mess. He was trying to figure out what the papers said when a co-worker walked by, "Oh-oh, I know what those are. Divorce papers. Do you have a lawyer?"

Mike looked up at the woman. At first he was irritated she read his private mail over his shoulder. But, almost immediately, the irritation disappeared. *Maybe she knew a lawyer who could help him figure out what to do with the papers?* "My wife is divorcing me for another guy. I just got these this morning and haven't a clue what they say."

"Well, if you'd like, I can give you the number of the attorney who handled my divorce. He really helped me when I needed him."

"That'd be great. He isn't expensive is he?"

"No, he only charged me $1,500, and he got me child support and half of everything. He's great!"

"Thanks. I guess I'm going to need an attorney to figure this out."

She gave him the number, and Mike called the lawyer. He made an appointment for the next day.

The meeting with the attorney went well. After looking at the divorce papers, the lawyer said they looked pretty good and only recommended making a few changes. He informed Mike he would draft the changes and send them to his wife's attorney. The best news was, it would only cost him $1,000.

When Friday came, Mike felt everything was going pretty well. He left work early and headed for the hospital. Kitty was waiting when he arrived. There was one problem before she could leave: she didn't have any clothes. When Mike heard, he laughed. What a silly problem to have.

"Don't laugh! I can't go around the city wearing a hospital gown! This is a serious problem, Mike."

"Okay, I'll go and get you some clothes. What do you want? Jeans and a top, or something else?"

Kitty thought for a moment. "I'm going to need everything: pants, tops, and underwear, just everything."

"Well, give me a list, with the sizes, and I'll pick up them up."

Two hours later, Mike returned with two outfits. After she was dressed, they left the hospital and headed for the apartment. Kitty was nervous, but Mike assured her it would be okay.

Mike's apartment was on the ground floor, and they entered through the patio doors. It was easier to go in that way than to try to maneuver through the front door because of the few steps. When they entered, Mike looked at Kitty expectantly. She looked around. Everything was clean and neat. The furniture was casual and spaced so she would be able to get around in her wheelchair. "Would you like to see the bedroom?" Mike asked tentatively.

Kitty nodded but didn't say anything.

He wheeled her around the corner and into the bedroom. Like the rest of the apartment, it was clean and neat with room for her to maneuver around. Mike looked at her expectantly.

Kitty looked around. She couldn't believe he had done all this just for her. The bedroom was decorated in bright and cheery pastel colors. It looked like a girl's room, which of course, it was.

Kitty looked up at Mike, "Where are you going to sleep?"

"Oh," he replied, "the sofa pulls out to a bed. I'll sleep there."

She felt tears begin flowing. She looked up at him and smiled.

He smiled back.

Everything was going to work out fine.

After a couple of days life began to fall into a routine for both of them. Mike went to work each day, and Kitty spent the day learning how to live as a paraplegic. It wasn't easy.

On the third day of living together, Mike remembered his conversation with the ICU nurse, Sandy. That night at dinner Mike broached the subject. "Do you remember the night you told me about Dr. Roth's decision not to do the surgery?"

Kitty nodded.

"Well, when I left I met Sandy in the parking lot. Do you remember Sandy, your nurse when you were in Intensive Care?"

Again, Kitty nodded. She didn't have a clue where Mike was going with this conversation.

"Well, she asked about you, and I told her about Dr. Roth's decision. She said wasn't surprised. She said he's a lousy doctor and pretty lazy. Then she gave me her home phone number and mentioned her husband is a neurosurgeon and might be able to help you." He pulled the slip of paper with Sandy's phone number out of his pocket and handed it to her. "She told me she would tell her husband about your case and he would be expecting your call, once you got out of the hospital."

As Kitty stared at the slip of paper, a spark of hope began to grow in her heart. She looked up at Mike, "Why didn't you tell me about this before?"

"Sandy asked me not to say anything until you were out of the hospital. She was worried if anyone at the hospital found out she gave you her phone number, she would get fired. I didn't tell you before now because I wanted you to have a chance to get acclimated to your new surroundings first."

Kitty nodded, "Do you think I should call her?"

"Yeah, I think you should, and the sooner the better."

"When should I call?"

Mike looked at her but didn't say anything.

"I mean, what time of day? Should I call in the morning or wait until after dinner?"

Mike replied, "I think after dinner would be best. In fact, I think you should call her now."

He got up, walked over, and picked up the phone. Walking back, he held it out to her. She looked at the handset and then at Mike. The look in his eyes was confident and assuring.

She took the phone and dialed the number.

CHAPTER 5

Detective Marcus Cooper sat at his desk with the case jacket sitting in front of him. He'd been a detective for fifteen years and still couldn't understand how someone could do something like this to another person. He picked up the jacket, opened it, and began reviewing the case notes.

Later, he left the office and drove to Washington Street where the assault happened. He looked around the crime scene again. There wasn't much to see, just a dirty alley with the usual amount of trash and debris. The yellow police line was still lying on the ground near the spot where Kitty was found.

He walked into the bar next to the alley. It was dark inside and took a few moments for his eyes to adjust. Cooper looked around and saw the typical seedy strip bar. There was loud music thudding from speakers all around the bar. Along the far wall was a stage lit with colored lights. On the stage, a bored looking young woman gyrated to the music. She was, of course, topless.

Cooper walked over to the bar and waited for the bartender to come over. When she did, Cooper leaned toward her, "Is there a manager on duty?"

The woman nodded and yelled back, "I'm the manager. What can I do for you?"

Cooper flashed his badge, "Is there somewhere we can go to talk?"

The woman looked around and motioned to another woman to take over for her. Then she motioned for Cooper to follow her and led him onto the stage and behind the curtains. At last they arrived at a small dingy office. When the manager closed the door, the sound level was reduced to a dull thudding. "What can I do for you, Officer," she asked moving behind an ancient looking desk.

Cooper looked around the tiny office. Even though it was small and dimly lit, it was clean and organized. He looked back at the woman, "My name is Detective Marcus Cooper. I'm investigating the sexual assault from the other night. Were you on duty that night?"

"Yeah, but I didn't see anything. I didn't leave the bar until after the girl was found."

"Do you recall anything unusual from that night? Were there any customers that stuck in your mind?"

"No, I don't think so." She paused for a moment. "Wait! There was a group of guys that come to mind. Yeah, I do remember them. They got drunk and rowdy. I finally had to throw them out."

Cooper took out his notebook and began scribbling. "Do you remember how many guys there were?"

"Yeah, there were four of them. I remember the ringleader. He was mean looking and really drunk. I remember when we threw them out, he threatened to come back and 'do me real good' whatever that meant. Anyway, he was a real asshole."

"Do you remember what he looked like?" Cooper asked as he continued writing.

"He was pretty big. You know, not real tall but big. He looked real strong too, kind of like he worked out or something."

"Can you describe him better than kind of big? Was he black, white, Hispanic, Asian? Did he have long or short hair? What color was his hair? What was he wearing? Did he have any tattoos? Can you remember any details of that sort?"

The manager thought about it for a few seconds. "He was white; about five feet eleven, two hundred fifty or sixty pounds. He had short blonde hair with mean, nasty, beady eyes. He was the kind of man that gives you the creeps, you know?"

"Do you think you would be recognize him if you saw him again?"

"Yeah, I sure would. I meet lots of weird guys here, but this guy really stuck in my head. Yeah, I'd know that dude anywhere."

"What about the other men in the group? Can you remember what any of them looked like?"

"No, none of the others stick out in my mind. They were pretty nondescript. I don't think any of them would have been a problem if it wasn't for the big mouthed leader."

"Do you know if there are any CCTV cameras in the area that may have filmed the alley that night?"

She smiled, "I was wondering if you were going to ask me that." She got up and walked over to a safe in the corner. After dialing in the combination, she opened the top drawer, picked up a video disc and handed it to Cooper. "This is the video recording from the camera in the back. It's looking at the back door, but it also covers a lot of the alley around it. I don't know exactly what it shows. I didn't look at it."

Cooper took the disc and placed it in his jacket pocket. He thanked her for her help, and after getting her name and phone number, left the bar.

When he got back to the station he watched the video. It showed the assault and the rape but from too far away to make clear identification. Also, the lighting was very poor, making the images grainy. Maybe forensics could enhance the film and get something useful from it.

Detective Cooper interviewed Kitty the day after he went to the bar. She told him what she could remember, which wasn't much. She remembered the name of the guy that had grabbed her was Al. And she remembered what he was wearing, but that was all.

When she was brought in to the emergency room, the police crime scene technicians were called. After they arrived, they collected evidence from the rape and her clothing. They also found evidence under her finger nails, skin and blood from where she scratched her attacker. It was all taken to the police crime lab for examination.

Detective Cooper received the lab report about two weeks later. The report identified the blood and tissue samples from under her finger nails belonged to a man named Alton St. James. Cooper looked at the man's record and saw that St. James had been arrested for sexual assault before, but he hadn't been convicted. There were plenty of other arrests on his record: armed assault, attempted burglary, and destruction of property, just to name a few of the charges.

The report also identified a man named Harold Myers. He had a record too, but it was a lot smaller than St. James's. Most of his prior arrests were for petty crimes such as Theft and Shoplifting.

He drove to the last known address for St. James, but he no longer lived there. There was no forwarding address. Next, he went to Myers's last known address. This time he got lucky. Myers still lived there. When

Myers answered the door, Cooper identified himself and asked if he could come in.

He could see Myers was nervous, but after a moment, he let him in. Myers led the way to the living room where Cooper was surprised to see an old woman sitting in front of an ancient TV. They sat down, and Myers said, "This is my mother, Jane."

Cooper nodded at the old woman, "Nice to meet you."

The old woman glared at him and turned back to the television.

"Can we go someplace else and talk? Someplace more private," Cooper asked Myers.

"Yeah, let's go into the kitchen. We won't be interrupted there."

As they sat at the kitchen table, Cooper looked at Myers, "I wanted to talk to you about an assault that happened on the night of the 14th on Washington Street, next to the Dance Slipper Bar."

Myers didn't say anything.

Cooper continued, "A young woman was beaten and sexually assaulted in the alley next to the bar. Would you know anything about it?"

Myers was sweating now. He didn't look at Cooper when he replied, "No, I don't know nothin' about no assaults."

Cooper wasn't surprised. "If it would help refresh your memory, it was a Monday night about three weeks ago around one A.M."

"Nope, doesn't ring a bell," Myers barked.

"The woman was eighteen, long blond hair, wearing blue jeans and a white tee shirt."

"I told you, I don't know nothin' about no assault. I'm not even sure I was at the Dance Slipper that night. Hell, I might have been home. I don't remember."

Sweat was pouring down Myers's face now. Cooper knew the man was lying. He decided to change directions. "Do you know a man named Alton St. James?"

Myers wiped his forehead with his sleeve. "Yeah, I know him. I've seen him around from time to time. I wouldn't call him a friend or anything."

"Do you know if he was at the Dance Slipper that night?"

"I don't know. I wasn't there."

"Mr. Myers, I have reason to believe you and Mr. St. James were involved in the assault of a young woman. I would like you to come down to the police station with me. Now, there are two ways we can do this. You can come down voluntarily, or I can get a warrant and bring you down in handcuffs. It's up to you."

Myers looked around the kitchen. His eyes darted all around the room, looking for something anything that could save him. There wasn't a thing. Cooper had seen that look before. He knew Myers was thinking about running, but before he had a chance to try, Cooper said, "Don't even think about bolting. You won't get far."

Myers's shoulders drooped. He looked defeated. Cooper had seen that look before too. He smiled to himself. Myers would tell him everything he wanted to know. Cooper got up and looked at Myers, "Come on. You can say goodbye to your mother on the way out."

Myers got up from the table and walked into the living room. He looked at his mother, "I'm going out for a while, Mom."

She didn't even look up as he left.

Once they arrived at the station, Cooper grabbed another detective. After briefing him, they took Myers into an interview room. With the video and audio recorders running, they began questioning Myers.

"Before we go any further, I want to advise you of your Constitutional rights," Cooper began. After reading him his Miranda Warning rights, Cooper introduced the other detective and began the interview. Three hours later, they had a confession.

Myers told the detectives he met St. James and a few of their mutual friends at a restaurant earlier in the evening. After dinner they decided to go bar hopping. The Dance Slipper was their seventh stop. By then most of them were pretty drunk. Myers explained when St. James got drunk, he got mean. The Dance Slipper wasn't the only bar they had been thrown out of that night. In fact, it was the third.

Once they were outside, they lit cigarettes and were trying to decide where to go next. That's when a young girl came walking down the street. St. James started making comments, and the girl looked scared. Just as the girl was hurrying past, Myers stated St. James grabbed her. According to Myers, when she slapped him, St. James went berserk. He punched her and slammed her into the wall. After, he got her on the ground, and they all took turns with her.

By the time Myers finished confessing, he was crying like a baby. He begged for forgiveness and claimed he never meant to hurt the girl. When he said he wished he could do something to make up for it, Cooper leaned toward him and said, "You can help her, Harold. You can turn state's evidence. Help us put away the other men who did this to her."

At the end of the interview, Cooper told Myers he was now going to be booked for First Degree Sexual Assault and First Degree Battery. He went on to explain if he cooperated, the district attorney would be willing to cut him a deal.

When Cooper got back to his office, he called the prosecutor's office to discuss the case. The case was assigned to Jennifer Greene, a young woman in the Sex Offence Office. It was her first case. When she heard the specifics of the case, she agreed to indict Myers and pursue an arrest warrant against St. James. She warned him not to go after St. James until the warrant was issued. She didn't want to spook him into going underground. Like she had to tell him that.

The last thing he did that day was to call Kitty and tell her the good news.

CHAPTER 6

Sandy picked up the phone on the second ring. "Hello."

Kitty found her mouth suddenly dry as a desert. She replied, "Hello, is this Sandy?"

"Yes."

"This is Kitty Benson. You were my nurse when I was in the Intensive Care Unit at City General."

"Oh, yes," she answered, "I remember you. You were the girl who was raped and beaten so badly that we didn't know if you would survive. How are you doing?"

"I'm fine," Kitty replied. She was nervous as she continued, "You met my friend Mike Hatfield in the parking lot and gave him your phone number. You told him your husband may be able to help me?"

There was silence on the other end of the line for a couple of seconds. Then Sandy said, "Oh yes, I do remember that. I suppose you called to talk to Ronnie, my husband?"

"If he has a few minutes, yes,"

"Well, I'd be glad to let you talk to him, but he's not here. He's at Mercy Hospital performing emergency surgery on a car accident victim. I don't know when he'll be back."

Kitty's heart sank. She hadn't realized it, but she was hoping against hope her paralysis would soon be over. Now she found her heart was broken again. She didn't know what to say.

"If you give me your number, I'll have Ronnie call you when he gets back, or tomorrow morning if he gets in too late tonight."

Kitty's heart went back to its old place. She gave Sandy the number and thanked her for her time. When she hung up the phone, Mike could see the disappointment in her face. He didn't know what to say but felt he had to say something. "What did she say?"

"She said her husband was in surgery and would call me back either tonight or tomorrow morning."

"Oh, that's not bad. If he's busy, that could mean he's really good."

"Yeah, but if he's really good, he might be too busy to see me."

"You worry too much. Let's just see what happens when he calls you back."

The rest of the evening Kitty was quiet. She tried to keep her spirits up but not to get too excited. After all, she told herself, he may not be able to help her. Even if he did agree to do the surgery, there was still a chance she would never walk again, and how was she going to pay for it?

Just then, the phone rang. Kitty's heart began to race as she picked it up. "Hello?"

There was silence on the other end of the phone for a few seconds. Once again Kitty said, "Hello?"

A woman's voice on the other end stammered, "Ah, is Mike there?"

"Yes, he is, hang on," Kitty handed the phone to Mike.

Mike had a quizzical look on his face as he took the phone. Kitty just shrugged.

"Hello?" he said.

"Who the hell was that!" demanded his wife.

"That," he replied, "is my new roommate, Kitty."

"Kitty, what kind of name is Kitty?" she asked sarcastically.

"Sharron, did you have a purpose in calling me, or did you just want to chat about my roommate?" Mike cut her off.

"Yes, I had a purpose. I was calling you to tell you your boys want to see you. They want to spend a few weeks with you this summer. I told them I would talk to you about it, but now I don't know if I should let them. How old is this girl?"

"First of all Sharron, Kitty is my roommate, not my lover. Her age is unimportant. If the boys want to spend a few weeks with me that will be fine, just let me know when."

"I'm not so sure I'm going to let them spend time with you and your...

ah roommate."

"You're one to talk! You found a new boyfriend and filed for divorce. And you're threatening not to let the kids visit me just because my roommate is a woman? You're being ridiculous!"

"At least I keep my love life private, if they come to visit you, you'll probably be screwing that girl right in front of them!"

"Sharron, stop!" Mike hissed. "Kitty is just a friend, not a lover. She's only eighteen, way too young for me. And believe it or not, I'm still in love with you! I haven't even begun to think about dating again."

There was silence on the other end. At last, Sharron said quietly, "You're still in love with me?"

Mike's voice quivered, "Yes, I am. I always have been, and I probably always will be. I can't help it."

"And there's nothing between you and that girl?"

"No, there's nothing between Kitty and me. She's around Chris's age, and I think of her like a daughter more than anything."

"I'm sorry, Mike. I don't know what got into me."

"Never mind," he dismissed her apology. "So, when are the boys wanting to visit?"

"Chris was thinking about driving up next month, if that's alright with you."

"That's fine. I'll see if I can get a few days off while they're here. Tell them I'm not sure how much time I can get off. I just started this job you know."

"I'll tell them. I'll let you know exactly when they're coming."

"Okay, I'll look forward to hearing from you." Without saying goodbye, Mike hung up the phone.

Throughout the conversation, Kitty tried not to listen. Even so, she couldn't help but hear what was being said. The longer the conversation went on, the worse she felt. By the time Mike hung up, she felt like she was coming between him and his family.

"Mike, I think I should look for somewhere else to live before your kids come. I don't want to cause any problems between you and your family."

"Kitty, don't be stupid. You're not causing any trouble. It's Sharron that's causing trouble. You know, it's funny. She's the one who left me for another guy, and now she's acting like a jealous wife. She's the one with the new lover, not me. She's the one who filed for divorce. I wanted to get back together. Now, it looks like she's trying to keep me from seeing the kids. What a piece of work!"

Kitty could tell Mike was getting wound up, and it just made her feel worse. "Still," she said, "I don't want to come between you and your family. I'll start looking for someplace to go tomorrow."

"The last thing I want or need is for you to leave. I like your company. I want you to stay. Please, don't talk about leaving at least until you talk to Sandy's husband about your back."

Kitty was silent, deep in her own thoughts.

Mike was silent too. He knew Kitty was feeling bad about what she had overheard. He never thought he would think it, but right now he hated Sharron for what she just did. Here was a vulnerable young girl trying to get her life back together after a vicious attack that left her in a wheelchair. On top of his anger, he now felt guilty for his feelings of hatred towards his wife.

For her part, Kitty was feeling guilty too. She thoroughly believed she was coming between Mike and his family. After all he'd done for her, she couldn't stand the thought of him and his wife arguing because of her. She didn't even want to think about what her presence might do to his relationship with his kids. No, all in all, she thought the best thing for everyone was for her to find another place to live. But, where would she go? She was stuck in a wheelchair, possibly for the rest of her life. She didn't have a job and no prospects of getting one either. *Maybe the best thing for her was to just go home.*

That was a great idea! She could just imagine her parents' expressions if she showed up in a wheelchair. If she thought they tried to run her life before, now it would be even worse. She was sure she would never be allowed to leave the house if she went home now. And Mom would have a field day. Within a week, Mom would have her convinced she wasn't capable of blowing her own nose without someone helping her. Worst of all, Mom would use the occasion to make herself out to be a martyr. Mom would put on a brave facade for the entire world to see. 'Look at me,' it would say, 'here I am stuck for the rest of my life caring for my irresponsible daughter who ran away from home and got herself attacked and paralyzed, but I'm dealing with it. I'm dealing with it.' *Yeah, that'd be great.*

And then there was her "holier than thou" father. He'd probably spend his time lecturing her on how she got what she deserved for being such a hellion. 'Sin in haste, repent in leisure,' he would say. 'This is what your disobedience has gotten you.' Karmic retribution, if he believed in Karma that is.

Still, there had to be someplace she could go. Somebody somewhere would help her, she was sure. But, where should she start looking? That was the big question she had to answer. She thought maybe the city had an agency that helped homeless people in wheelchairs. *Yes, that was it!* She'd call the city government tomorrow while Mike was at work. And, if she was lucky, she'd be long gone before his kids showed up.

But what about Mike's statement that he wanted her to stay, that he needed her to stay? Was he telling the truth or was he just saying that to make her feel better about mooching off of him? Part of her felt he was just being nice but then she remembered even before she was attacked he offered her the chance to use his motel room. Maybe he was telling the truth. *Maybe he did need her, but what for?* She just couldn't figure that out, at least not yet.

It was all too confusing, and she didn't want to think about it anymore. She decided she was tired. It wasn't late but she found she got tired easily these days. She looked over at Mike, "I think I'll go to bed now, goodnight."

Mike was lost deep in thought. When she spoke, he came out of his revelry, "What? Oh yeah, goodnight."

He watched as she wheeled herself to the bedroom but wasn't really paying attention. He wondered why life seemed so complicated. *Oh well, maybe life is supposed to be that way.* He decided to go to bed too.

The next day, after Mike left for work, the phone rang. It took Kitty five rings to get to the phone. *This wheelchair is really a pain,* she thought. She picked up the phone, "Hello?"

"Is Miss Kitty Benson there?" the voice on the other end asked.

"This is she." Kitty replied.

"This is Dr. Boyd's office calling," a woman's voice confirmed. "Dr. Boyd asked me to set up an appointment for you for later this week. When are you available to come in?"

It took Kitty a second to realize it must be Sandy's husband's office calling. Her heart was in her throat as she said, "What do you have available?"

"We have 2:30 PM tomorrow afternoon, 9:45 Wednesday morning and 12 noon on Friday."

Kitty thought for a moment. "Can I call you back? I have to call my friend to see if he can get off work to drive me. I'm in a wheelchair and don't have any way to get there."

"Oh," said the woman, "That will be fine."

"Can you give me your phone number? I'll call you back in a few minutes."

The woman gave the number and hung up. Kitty called Mike and explained about the call. Mike told her he would check with his supervisor and call her back in a few minutes. Kitty hung up the phone.

No sooner had she put the phone down than it began ringing again. She picked it up, "Hello?"

A man's voice spoke, "This is Dr. Boyd, is this Miss Benson?"

Kitty was slightly confused when she answered, "Yes it is."

"It's Kitty isn't it?" Without waiting for a response, he continued. "Kitty, my wife, Sandy, told me about your case and asked me to see if I could help. When I had Molly call you about making an appointment, she forgot to mention we could send someone to pick you up. Sandy told me you were in a wheelchair and would probably have a hard time getting here."

Kitty didn't know what to say. After a second or two she said, "That's very kind of you."

Dr. Boyd laughed, "Don't think I do this for every patient. It's just Sandy can be very persuasive." After a brief pause he added, "So, when can you come in?"

Kitty didn't hesitate, "Whenever you like."

"Great! How about tomorrow at 2:30?"

"That'd be fine," she answered, still stunned at her good fortune.

"Great, let me get your address. A van will pick you up at 2."

After she recited the address, he said, "Okay, I'll see you then," and hung up.

Kitty immediately called Mike and told him the good news.

"That's great," Mike said, "because I couldn't get off. There's a big staff meeting tomorrow. I can't miss it."

CHAPTER 7

The next afternoon there was a knock on the door. Kitty wheeled herself to the door and opened it. Standing in front of her was the man who had attacked her. She screamed and slammed the door, throwing the bolt across it as fast as she could. She hurriedly wheeled herself to the phone and dialed 9-1-1.

When the dispatcher answered, Kitty was panicking. "9-1-1 what is your emergency," the voice said.

"The man who raped and beat me is at my front door!" Kitty screamed into the phone.

"Calm down, ma'am, I can't understand you," the dispatcher said. "Who's at your door and where are you?"

There was a loud banging on the door as Kitty said, "My name is Kitty Benson. I live at 2325 West Pickett Street, Apartment 1C. The man who raped and beat me is trying to break my door down!"

The dispatcher was typing on her computer. As she typed she asked, "Can you describe the man?"

"He's big and tall and in a gray uniform. Please hurry."

"The police are on their way ma'am. Stay on the line with me until they arrive."

Al hated his job, driving invalids around town for twelve bucks an hour. Most of them could barely speak, and none of them could move. *It was disgusting*, he thought. They should all be put in an institution or killed; he didn't care which.

It was just after lunch when he was dispatched to pick up a woman in a wheelchair on West Pickett. The dispatcher told him the woman's name, but it didn't ring a bell. He figured it was just some old bitty who needed a ride to the doctor's office for a prescription. Maybe he'd be asked to take her to the pharmacy, and she would pick up some pain pills he could steal from her. *That'd be cool*, he thought.

When he knocked on the door, he never expected to see the alley girl. As the door opened his heart skipped a couple of beats. It was her: the bitch he beat up months ago! What if she recognized him? What if she called the police?

When she screamed and slammed the door in his face, he knew he had to do something to shut the bitch up. He began banging on the door. It was a steel door and didn't budge when he kicked it. The only thing he was doing was hurting his fists and foot. He decided he needed to try something else.

He ran out the front door and turned right. He started looking into the patio doors. *She had to be here somewhere,* he thought. Panic was rising in his chest when he finally found the right patio. Through the glass he could see she was on the telephone, probably with the police. He was running towards the glass doors when he heard the sirens. He skidded to a stop. *Time to make an exit,* he thought, running to his van. He jumped in, put it in drive, and spun the tires as he made his get-a-way.

When the banging stopped, Kitty thought the guy had run away. She just started to calm down when she saw him outside the patio sliding glass door. The poor dispatcher's eardrum must have ruptured as Kitty screamed into the phone, "He's at the patio door! Oh God, hurry! He's gonna to kill me!"

As he started running towards the door, Kitty screamed again. She watched in terror before he suddenly stopped and ran away. She couldn't take her eyes off him as he ran to a van, jumped in, and sped off.

All the time she was screaming into the phone. The dispatcher couldn't understand much of what she was saying, but she got the gist of it. As she listened to the drama being played out on the other end of the phone, the dispatcher kept typing. She knew the responding units would need all the information they could get, and it was her job to give it to them.

The first police car to arrive actually drove through the cloud of smoke from the van's tires. The officer jumped out and raced to the front door of the apartment building, his gun drawn. When he didn't find anyone at the door, he sprinted to the patio. By then there were four police cars in the parking lot.

A middle age man with sergeant's stripes on his sleeves knocked on the patio door. Kitty, still on the phone, wheeled herself to the door and opened it. Once the sergeant assured her the man was gone, she hung up the phone. The sergeant called one of the officers over and told her to take notes as he asked Kitty questions.

Detective Cooper heard the call go out on his portable radio. He couldn't believe what he was hearing. As soon as he heard the specifics, he sprinted to his car. With lights and siren blaring, he raced to the address Dispatch had given. Even after units arrived, he continued racing to the scene.

He arrived only minutes after the other units. He jogged to the open door and saw Kitty, nearly hysterical telling the officers what had happened. As he walked over to her, she recognized him. She grabbed his jacket, pulled it to her face, and began crying into it. He put his arm around her neck and began telling her everything was going to be alright. The sergeant looked at him, and Cooper explained he was the investigator on her assault case.

Once Kitty calmed down sufficiently, Cooper asked, "How do you think he found out where you were?"

Through her sniffles, Kitty said, "I have a doctor's appointment, and I was expecting someone to pick me up. When the doorbell rang, I opened the door expecting the driver to be here. Only, it was him."

She began crying again, and Cooper patted her gently. As he was patting her back, he asked, "What's the name of the company that's supposed to pick you up?"

"I don't know. The doctor's office arranged for the van."

"Do you have the doctor's office number?"

Kitty gave him the number, and stepping outside, he called it.

Al knew he couldn't go back to the office. He'd have to ditch the van somewhere and get out of town before the cops could put it all together and come after him. He'd have to get some other clothes too. There was no way he could get his things from his locker at work. He slowed down and headed for his apartment.

He parked the van a block away, just in case someone got his license number when he left that bitch's apartment. He hurried into his apartment and began stripping off the uniform even before the door closed. He put on a pair of jeans and a polo shirt and then began packing a few things into an old gym bag. Ten minutes later he was back in the van.

He drove to the far side of town and pulled into an alley about three blocks from the bus station. He left the keys in the ignition as he hurried away. At the bus station, he bought a ticket to a city in the next state and waited. He was either going to get away, or they would try to pick him up here. If they did try to arrest him, he had a surprise just waiting for them.

It only took Cooper a few minutes to get the phone number for the transport company from the doctor's office and a few more to get the name of the driver dispatched to pick Kitty up. He called central dispatch, gave them the name and a brief description, and headed back into the apartment.

Kitty was still talking to the female officer when he walked in. "Kitty, I have good news. We now know the name of the man and have his address. I'm sending a car over there to look for him. If we're lucky, he'll be in jail by tonight."

"You're not leaving me here alone are you?" she pleaded.

"Of course not, someone will stay with you until you can call someone."

"The only person I can call is Mike, and he's in a meeting." Tears began to flow down her cheeks again.

"Alright, don't worry we aren't going to leave you alone. We'll leave an officer posted outside until Mike gets home from work. In the meantime, I'm going to have to leave you now. I've got to go check out this guy's apartment."

The female officer who'd been taking notes was assigned to stay with Kitty until Mike got home from work. While they were waiting, the two women got to know each other better. The policewoman's name was Michelle D'Angelo. She was new to the force, having just graduated from the academy. She and Kitty talked for a few minutes before Kitty's attack came up. Kitty told her the basics, and Michelle didn't ask questions.

While he was walking back out to his car, Cooper called Mike in his office. "Mr. Hatfield, this is Detective Cooper. Have you got a minute?"

"Yes, of course. What's up?" Mike replied.

"There was a bit of a problem at your apartment this afternoon," Cooper began. "Ms. Benson was almost attacked by the man she says assaulted her. It seems he's employed by a handicap transport company and was dispatched to pick her up for her doctor's appointment. Once he recognized her, he tried to break in, but the police arrived before he could."

"Oh my God!" Mike exclaimed. "Is Kitty alight?"

"She's pretty shook up, as I'm sure you can imagine. I've left a policewoman with her so she's not alone. The officer will stay until you get home so you needn't worry. But the reason I'm calling you is... Until we catch this guy, she's going to be a nervous wreck. That's going to be the real problem."

"What do you think I should do?" Mike asked.

"I don't know. Is there a neighbor you know that can look in on Kitty from time to time? Maybe there's somewhere she can go while you're at work? I don't know. That's for you and her to decide. Anyway, I thought you needed to know. Listen, I've got to go. I've got to interview this sleazebag's boss. I'll talk to you later."

"Okay, Detective. Thanks for the call." Mike hung up the phone. He walked over to his boss's office and told her what happened. He needed to go home, now.

When he got back to the apartment, Kitty was talking to the policewoman, Michelle. Kitty was obviously still upset but had calmed down quite a bit. When Mike opened the door, he could see the fear in her eyes until she recognized him. When she did, she wheeled herself over to him and hugged him tightly. "Oh Mike, I'm so glad you're home."

Mike held on firmly, "Thank God you're okay! What happened?"

As Kitty told her story, Michelle got up and prepared to leave. Once Kitty finished, Mike looked at Michelle, "Thank you so much for staying with her, Officer. I can't tell you how relieved I was to hear you were here."

Michelle smiled, "That's okay, I enjoyed being here." She blushed and added, "I guess I shouldn't have said that, given the circumstances. What I meant was, I enjoyed being here with Miss Benson."

Kitty smiled, "Thank you so much, Michelle. I really appreciate you staying with me. I enjoyed our talk too."

"You know," Michelle began, "I'll be off on Thursday and Friday. Maybe, if you feel like it, we could go shopping or something. That is, if you're up to it?"

"That's a great idea," Mike agreed. "That way, you won't be alone, and I won't have to worry about you while I'm at work."

Kitty shook her head, "I don't want you to feel like you have to do that. You've done enough staying with me till Mike got home. I don't want to take up your days off too."

"Really, it's no problem. I'm new here, so I don't have many friends and not much to do on my days off anyway. Besides, it'll be fun having another girl to hang out with. Most of the women on the force are married and spend their off time with their husbands and kids. The guys on the force are usually interested in hanging out with a single lady for one thing."

"Yeah, tell me about it," Kitty joked. "Sometimes, I think that's all guys are interested in."

Mike faked affronted, "Hey, that's not fair. I'm not that way."

All three laughed. The tension seemed to melt like ice in the summertime.

"Well, I need to get back to the station and finish my paperwork. I'll call you Thursday morning. Okay?"

"Sounds good. Thanks" Kitty replied.

After Michelle left, Mike and Kitty looked at each other. "Are you hungry?" he finally asked.

Kitty was surprised to find that she was. She nodded. "Okay, why don't we go somewhere and get dinner. What do you feel like, Chinese?"

"That sounds good," Kitty agreed.

As they were heading for the door, the phone rang. Mike sighed before answering, "Hello?"

"This is Dr. Boyd's office," a woman stated. "Is Miss Benson there?"

"Yes, one moment," Mike handed Kitty the phone.

"Hello?"

"This is Dr. Boyd's office. We were calling to find out why you missed your appointment."

"Oh," Kitty took a deep breathe. "It's a long story, but basically, the man who attacked me weeks ago was the driver for the transportation company you sent to pick me up."

"Oh, my God!" she exclaimed. "Are you okay?"

"Yeah, I'm fine, now." Kitty replied. "The police came. In fact, they just left. The appointment completely slipped my mind because of everything."

"Thank God you're alright. Well, I guess we'll reschedule your appointment to 9:45 Wednesday morning?"

"That will be fine. Are you going to arrange for transportation again?" Kitty asked.

"Yes, of course. Only, this time, we'll use a different company."

"I don't think you need to worry about that," Kitty said. "I don't think that guy will be working for them anymore."

After hanging up the phone, Kitty and Mike went to dinner.

Al was antsy waiting for the bus to load. Every few seconds he looked around, hoping against hope he could escape before getting caught. After what seemed like hours, the final announcement came. Al breathed a sigh of relief, got up, and started walking towards the door that led to freedom. As his eyes raked the waiting room, he saw two uniformed police officers walk in.

He ducked down and walked as quickly as he could without running toward the buses. He almost made it. He was only a few feet from the station door when one of the officers elbowed his partner and pointed at him.

The two cops yelled something and started running toward him. Al didn't hesitate. He ran dead out through the door and dodged left. The police officers gave chase. They chased Al two blocks and down an alley before finally losing him. Al ducked into the back door of a theater and hid behind the screen for over an hour. When the movie ended, he joined the crowd leaving out the front door. Thankfully, there were no police officers waiting. Al got away.

CHAPTER 8

For the next couple of days, the police beefed up their patrols around the apartment complex. Detective Cooper told Mike the patrol commander agreed to patrol their parking lot two or three times a shift for the next few days. This information made Mike and Kitty feel better, but she was still on edge when Mike went to work the next day.

When Mike came home that first night, he told Kitty his oldest son called and would be there the next week. Kitty still felt guilty she'd be there when his kids visited, but Mike told her to put it out of her mind, she had plenty of other things to worry about. Besides, his kids were going to love her anyway.

Thursday morning after Mike went to work, Kitty cleaned up the kitchen and was just having her second cup of coffee when there was a knock on the door. Startled, Kitty put her coffee cup down and rolled towards the door, stopping to grab the cordless phone on the way. As she reached the door, there was another knock and a voice said, "Kitty, are you there? It's me, Michelle D'Angelo."

Kitty let out the breath she hadn't realized she was holding and opened the door. Michelle smiled down at her. She looked very different than the last time Kitty had seen her. Instead of a uniform, Michelle wore a loose-fitting T-shirt and a pair of cut off jean shorts. Her hair was loose, and it made her look much younger, Kitty thought.

"Hi, are you ready or did you forget our shopping date today," Michelle asked.

"Oh, no, I didn't forget," Kitty said, "I just kind of lost track of time." Then, she added, "Come in. I'll get ready, it'll only take me a couple of minutes."

As Michelle walked in and sat down on the couch Kitty asked, "Would you like a cup of coffee or something?"

"Coffee would be great."

"Do you like cream or sugar, or both?"

"Just cream, thanks," Michelle replied.

Kitty handed her the coffee and she asked, "So where are we going?"

Michelle took a sip, "I thought we'd go to the mall and hang out for a while. I figured you might like going to the day spa and get some pampering. Then, maybe we'd get a couple of new outfits. Lunch and back here. Tomorrow, I thought we might go to the pool or maybe the gym for a few hours, if that's okay with you."

"That sounds great, but I don't think I can afford all that. Mike gave me some money, but not enough to pay for all that."

"Oh, it's okay. The spa usually gives me a big discount. I've got a coupon for a free makeover that I got for my last birthday you can use, so it won't cost you a dime. That way, you can use your money for the clothes. Lunch is on Detective Cooper. When I told him we were going to hang out at the mall today, he offered to buy lunch. And if there's one thing I learned in the academy, it's never turn down a free lunch," she said laughing.

"Are you sure? I don't want to take your birthday present. It wouldn't be right."

"Don't worry about it. I get one each year from my mom. The spa is a chain, and there's one in my hometown. Anyway, it's no big deal. Mom runs the spa back home, so she gets it free."

They left the apartment a half hour later and headed to the spa. Once there, Kitty had a great time. She got a pedicure, a manicure, and a facial. Michelle even talked her into a full body massage. Even though she couldn't feel it, she figured it might help keep her muscles alive. She was in for a surprise.

About half way through the massage, she began feeling something in her legs. Just as with her hands, she began feeling a slight tingling. She was excited when she told the masseuse, but told herself not to get too excited. It may have been just her imagination, but the masseuse recommended she tell her doctor anyway.

After the spa, they went to lunch at a restaurant in the mall followed by shopping the rest of the day. Kitty bought a bathing suit, just in case they went swimming at the pool the next day and three other outfits. Michelle bought two outfits, a bikini, and two pairs of shoes. At last it was time to head home.

They got to the apartment just before Mike did. When he walked in Michelle was drinking a glass of wine and laughing. When Mike asked how their day went, Kitty showed him everything she bought. Dinner consisted of salad and French bread. That night, as she was getting into bed, Kitty realized the tingling in her legs was still there.

Friday was spent at the apartment complex's pool. The two women arrived just after 1 PM and spent over an hour swimming and splashing around before they decided to sunbathe. While they were lounging, two men came over and began flirting with them, but after about fifteen minutes, they left. Even though the men didn't stay long, the encounter was a big boost to Kitty's ego. At the end of the day, the ladies decided to get together again the next time they had the chance.

"Thank you so much for the last couple days, Michelle. I really enjoyed hanging out with another girl," Kitty began.

"Yeah, it was fun. We should do it again sometime. I'll give you a call," Michelle said heading toward the parking lot.

"Absolutely!"

Al had spent the last two days sleeping in alleys and dodging passing police cars. He knew it couldn't last. Sooner or later, he'd get caught if he didn't get out of town. But every time he went by the train or bus station, there were always cops patrolling the entrance. He couldn't get inside to buy a ticket to get out of town.

He tried calling a few friends, but most of them told him they couldn't help him because the police were watching them. He doubted all of them were being watched. Yet, nothing he said could convince them to help. Finally, he decided to hitchhike out of town.

He walked up the ramp to the interstate and stuck out his thumb, hoping to make it to the coast. After about twenty minutes, a car pulled over to pick him up. He ran up and opened the passenger's door, "Thanks, I really appreciate this."

As Al sat down and pulled the door closed, the driver said, "No problem, dude, where ya goin'?"

"I don't care," Al replied, "Anywhere far away from here is good for me. Where are you headed?"

"I'm only going to the next town, dude," he said, "Gotta friend who's gonna hook me up. Ya know what I mean?"

They sped down the freeway, going faster and faster. Al glanced over at the speedometer and was shocked to see they were going over a hundred miles an hour. He was just about to say something when the driver cursed, "Damn, the five-oh," and began slowing down.

Al felt trapped. Looking behind them, he saw a police car with red and blue strobes flashing. The whole time the driver cursed under his breath as he slowed down and began to pull over.

Don't panic, he told himself. *They don't know who you are. This isn't your car and you're not driving so they won't care about you at all.* He was just calming down when the car came to a full stop on the shoulder of the road.

The officer couldn't believe it. Not even an hour into her shift and she had her first high speed stop. As she was following the car, she ran the license plates and let the dispatcher know where they were pulling over and how many people were in the car she was stopping.

She got out of her cruiser and walked up to the driver's window, stopping just behind it. When she asked the driver for his license and registration for the car, she looked over at the passenger. *That guy seems very nervous,* she thought to herself, *he keeps looking at his lap, not looking around at all.* She took the driver's information and walked back to her cruiser.

As the computer displayed the driver's information, she began writing his ticket. A bit of motion in front of her caught her eye. She looked up and saw the passenger's door opening. She picked up the public address microphone and told the man to get back into the car. He didn't comply. She put down her ticket book and got out of the car. As she walked toward the car, she continued telling passenger to get back into the car.

Unfortunately, Al was convinced she'd recognized him when she left the driver's side of the car to return to her patrol car. He remembered her looking over at him. He decided he couldn't take the chance the officer recognized him would be calling for back-up. When he opened his door, he intended to walk away. But the officer ordered him back into the car. *Well, the idea of walking away was no longer an option,* he thought grimly. He turned and walked toward the cop car.

By the time the officer got out of her car, he was at the back of his. She walked to the front of her car and confronted him. "Sir," she demanded, "Get back in the car now, or I'll have to arrest you."

As he continued walking towards her, she drew her gun and pointed it at him. He grabbed the barrel of the gun and pulled it towards him. "Shoot!" he bellowed.

She hesitated. In that moment of delay, he reached out and tugged on the gun. Simultaneously, he started spinning around, hoping to pull the gun out of her hands, but she didn't let go. Around and around he turned, the officer still hanging on yelling for him to let go. Finally, he slammed his body into hers, pushing her against the push bar on the front of her patrol car. She cried out in pain and let the gun go.

Without wasting any time, Al turned the gun on the officer and pulled the trigger. The first bullet hit her in the hip, and she went down. The second bullet hit her ballistic vest, and the third grazed her head, knocking her unconscious. Al stepped over the officer and kicked her onto her back. Then he reached down and grabbed the extra magazines from the officer's belt and walked back toward the man in the car who'd picked him up.

The driver ducked down when he heard the shots. After a few seconds, he looked up to see the hitchhiker at his window. He was pointing the policewoman's gun at him. Before he could say anything, the hitchhiker demanded, "Get out of the car."

"Dude," he questioned, "What are you doing?"

Al fired the gun for the fourth time that morning. The bullet hit the man in the shoulder. He screamed, "Alright, alright, just don't shoot me again, Dude!"

Al wrenched the door open and pulled the driver out. He screamed as Al pulled on his injured arm. "Hey, man," he shouted. "What do you think you're doing?"

Al got behind the wheel, slammed the car into drive, and sped off.

The wounded ex-driver stumbled back toward the police car. He grabbed the officer's radio microphone and screamed, "Help! There's a cop shot here. I don't know if she's dead or not. I've been shot too! Send help, please!!"

Meanwhile, Al turned on the radio and selected an all-news station. The traffic reporter was explaining the freeway was closed because of a cop being shot. While he described the scene as seen from his helicopter, Al realized he wouldn't get very far in the stolen car. He'd have to ditch it soon. He took the second exit off the freeway, drove a few blocks, parked the car in an abandoned garage, and walked away.

After pocketing the cop's gun, he walked a few blocks and went into a bar. The TV was showing a special report about the cop's shooting. The reporter was interviewing another cop who described Al and the car he stole. Al sat down in a dark corner booth and ordered a boilermaker, keeping his head down.

CHAPTER 9

Mike and Kitty had just finished their Sunday brunch and were talking about what they were going to do that day when there was a knock on the door. Mike walked over and peering through the peep hole saw his two sons. He flung open the door and took both kids in a giant bear hug. "Chris! Mikey! It's good to see you!" he exclaimed as he dragged them into the apartment.

Both boys returned the hug as they walked in. When Mike released them, they looked around. Chris was the first to comment, "Wow Dad, this place is kinda cool."

"Yeah Dad, it looks like a pretty nice place," Mikey agreed. Then, spotting Kitty he said, "This must be your friend Mom told us about."

Mike glanced at Kitty, "Boys, I'd like you to meet Kitty Benson. Kitty, these are my sons. This is Chris, he's the oldest. And this is Mike Jr., we call him Mikey."

Kitty smiled shyly, "It's nice to meet you."

Mikey and Chris walked over and sat at the table, smiling at her. "So, how long have you known Dad," Chris began.

"Not very long," she said. "We only met a couple of months ago."

"Don't stop there. Tell us more." Mikey continued.

For the next few minutes, Kitty told them how she and Mike met and what Mike had done for her since then. When she finished Chris sucked in a big breath, "Wow, Dad! She makes you sound like a saint or something."

Mike chuckled, "Oh, I'm no saint, Chris. I'm sure your mother has told you that."

They sat around the table and chit-chatted for a while. At first, Kitty was quiet and reserved, but after a while, she opened up and joined the conversation. By the evening, she felt as if she had known the boys her whole life.

Her fist impression of Mike's children was that they looked a lot like

Mike. But, after a while she decided Chris must look more like his mother. Where Mike had dark hair and brown eyes, Chris had light brown, almost blonde hair with light blue eyes. Mike was tall and thin while Chris was shorter and stockier, not fat, just barrel chested. Mikey, on the other hand, was a carbon copy of his father, right down to the mannerisms and his smile. They both seemed to have the same sense of humor and even the same style of talking.

They both were cute, but Kitty thought Chris was cuter. She couldn't keep her eyes off of him, and every time he caught her looking at him, she'd blush. Part of her couldn't believe she was attracted to a guy, especially after what had happened to her.

Chris kept glancing at Kitty whenever he thought she wasn't looking. The only thing was, she seemed to be always looking at him. *Did she feel the attraction he felt? If she did, what would Dad say if they got together? Better yet, what would Mom say?* Mom was convinced Dad was having an affair with this girl, but after meeting her, Chris didn't believe it. She just didn't seem the type of girl that would be interested in a man Dad's age.

After dinner, they gathered in the living room area and watched a movie. When it was over, Mike said, "Okay gang, tomorrow's a work day. It's midnight so I think we should call it a night. Chris, you and Mikey are going to have to use the sleeping bags I bought for you. They're in the coat closet. There should be room between the couch and the dining table for both of you. But if you don't like that idea, then I guess one of you can use the kitchen floor."

Al left the bar just before it closed. He staggered a bit as he walked down the street wondering where he was going to spend the night. As he rounded a corner he saw the answer to his quandary. The neon light flashing above the entrance said, "M_TEL." The place looked cheap and sleazy, but it beat a local alley.

Detective Cooper left the hospital about midnight. The officer was going to be alright, and the other victim had already been released. He hadn't learned much about the assailant except he seemed to matched the description of Alton St. James. But Cooper wasn't 100% sure. He'd have to show both the officer and the civilian victim a photo line-up tomorrow.

Mike woke to his alarm clock on Monday morning. He got up and maneuvered his way around his sons, went to the kitchen and made his coffee. Just as it finished brewing, Chris woke up. They sat at the table talking and drinking coffee until it was time for Mike to go to work. *It was good having his sons with him*, he thought. It reminded him of life before he lost his job and his family had left him. It was a nice feeling.

Kitty woke up and wheeled herself out of the bedroom just in time to say good-bye to Mike as he left for work. Mikey got up and the three of them ate breakfast and made plans for the day. There wasn't much to do she told them. They could choose between going to the pool or hanging around the apartment.

Mikey said, "Maybe that's all you can do without a car, but we've got wheels. We can go anywhere we want and do whatever we want since Chris has his car."

Chris ventured, "I've got an idea. Why don't we hang out at the pool, and then, after lunch, go to a movie. There's got to be a theater around here someplace."

They all agreed and quickly changed into their bathing suits. They spent the morning splashing around the pool. The boys helped Kitty in and out of the water and onto the lounger for a little sunbathing. She was s little embarrassed to have two cute guys carrying her to and from the water, but they didn't seem to mind.

Chris couldn't believe how light and soft Kitty felt. She was so light, he really didn't need Mikey's help but he figured he'd better let him help, so it wouldn't look like he was interested in her. *Was he interested in her? She certainly was cute enough*, he thought.

Mikey could see Chris and Kitty couldn't keep their eyes off of one another. He could also see neither one of them wanted the other to know. *How stupid*, he thought. *If you like someone, why not let them know?* Still, it was funny watching those two checking each other out.

Al left the motel and started walking, not really going anywhere. He had nowhere to go and all the time in the world to get there. After wandering around the neighborhood, he decided to head downtown to hang out. Maybe he'd see someone he knew, and they could get a drink or something to eat together. He started walking a little quicker. Even so, it took him a long time to get downtown. It was a long walk and every time he saw a police car, he ducked down an alley or turned and walked the other direction. He knew every cop in town would be looking for him.

Detective Cooper stopped by the hospital and showed the officer a photo spread with St. James's picture in the middle. As soon as she saw him, she pointed him out, "That's him. That's the guy who shot me."

"Are you sure?" he asked.

She said she'd know him anywhere.

Chalk another one up to St. James. He had graduated from the petty crimes he started with, Cooper thought. *He must be getting desperate.*

The next stop was the civilian carjacking victim. When he showed him the photo spread, he too picked St. James out in less than a second.

Two for two, thought Cooper, *Now all I have to do is find him.*

Back at the station, Cooper had St. James's picture reproduced and given to every patrol unit in the city with instructions to beat the bushes and make this guy surface. Maybe they'd get lucky and someone would recognize and turn him in. Then, he could close both cases.

When Mike got home he found the two boys and Kitty making dinner. Watching them interact, Mike thought they seemed like they knew each other their entire lives. Funny, he felt that way too.

Al made it downtown just after sunset. He went by most of his old hang outs but didn't stop. By now, the cops would know everyplace he liked to go and would have talked someone into calling them if he showed up. *No, really he didn't want to go in any of those places,* he was just hoping to see one of his buddies coming out or going in. Maybe, he'd get them to go someplace different with him. Maybe, if he was lucky, they'd pay for some food and perhaps help him hide somewhere. *Yeah, right, like that was going to happen! More than likely his buddies would turn him over to the cops in a second, especially if there was a reward.*

The next day was Kitty's doctor's appointment. She woke up before anyone else, dressed, and was making coffee when Mike got up for work. Soon, all four of them were sitting at the table talking. Mike noticed Kitty wasn't saying much and figured she must be nervous about today. "What time's the van coming to get you," he asked.

"I don't know," she replied. "My appointment is at 9:45 so I guess they'll be here by 9:30, but I'm not sure."

Chris spoke up, "Why don't Mikey and I take you? That way you won't have to worry about being late. Do you know where the doctor's office is?"

Kitty replied, "No, I don't. But, if you're serious, I can call and get directions. If you take me, I should probably call and cancel the van."

"Yeah, that'll work," Chris said. "We don't have anything to do today, and it'll be really boring without you around."

Kitty blushed, "Okay, I'll call the doctor after eight and get directions."

Mike chuckled as he left for the office. He could tell Chris and Kitty liked each other, even if they didn't want anyone to know.

The doctor's office was empty when they arrived and the doctor saw Kitty right away. After inviting her into the office, he began "First, we need to get another MRI. Then we'll see where we are. Have you had any pain or other sensations below your chest since you left the hospital?"

After she told him about the pins and needles she felt in her legs after the massage, he smiled and told her that was a hopeful sign.

The nurse wheeled her in for her MRI and, after an hour, back into Dr. Boyd's office. She waited over twenty minutes before the doctor came in. "I'm sorry," he apologized as he walked over and sat behind his desk.

Kitty's heart felt like it had stopped. *Did that mean he couldn't help her?*

"I didn't mean to keep you waiting that long. The last patient took longer than expected," he continued.

Kitty's heart began beating again.

"Now, let's take a look at your MRI, shall we?"

He pulled the CD out of its protective cover, swiveled around, and inserted it into the drive on his computer. As he looked at it, Kitty wheeled herself around the desk for a closer look. He glanced over at her and smiled. "This isn't as bad as I expected," he stated. "Look here," he pointed at the screen, "See the ruptured disc. See how it's pressing against the spinal cord?"

She nodded.

He continued, "It looks worse than it really is. In fact, I think once we remove it, you should eventually regain most, if not all, of the use of your lower extremities. Really, this is good news."

Kitty was relieved. She smiled when he looked at her, and he smiled back.

Dr. Boyd continued, "Now, I know you don't have any insurance or money to pay for the operation, but my surgical team will perform the operation pro bono. I should be able to talk the hospital into donating the operating room and supplies or at least connecting you with their Charity Care Program to pay for it. It might take me a while to schedule everything, but I should be able to arrange something before the end of the next month, maybe sooner.

"I don't want to get your hopes up too high Kitty. There's a chance the operation won't work, but I have every reason to believe it will. You'll have to stay in the hospital for a few days and after that ,you'll need physical therapy to fully regain the use of your legs. You may regain feeling in your legs as soon as you wake up, but it's not uncommon for it to take a day or two before you can feel anything. I tell you this now so you won't be upset if you wake up and don't feel anything different. Also, it's been a while since you've been able to use your legs, it will take time to strengthen the muscles before you can walk. But, don't lose faith. Everything should turn out okay in the long run." He paused, "Do you have any questions?"

"No. I think I understand," she answered. Hope filled her for the first time.

CHAPTER 10

Al was out of money and hungry. He hadn't slept in a bed for over a week and was getting desperate when he walked into the store. It was a little mom and pop store on the corner of a rundown residential section in an old part of town. He didn't think there would be much money, but he needed whatever he could get.

He browsed around the shelves until the last customer left. As he approached the counter, he pulled his cap down and his t-shirt over the bottom of his face. He drew the cop's gun and pointed it at the old Korean woman behind the cash register. "Money, now!" he growled.

The woman froze. "I no speak English," she blurted.

He didn't believe her. He struck her across the cheek with the barrel of the gun. Blood spurted from the gash. He bellowed, "Money, now!"

She cried out in pain at the gash opened on her cheek. With one hand trying to stem the flow of blood, she opened the cash register with the other. She pulled out ones, fives and tens and handed them to him. He looked down and saw there was only about fifty dollars there.

He looked up at her and said, "The twenties, underneath the tray. Now!"

"Me, no speak English," she cried again.

He pointed the gun over her shoulder and pulled the trigger. The roar beside her ear was deafening. "The twenties or the next one will be in your head!" he roared. "Now!"

She lifted the tray out and pulled out all the twenties, even a couple of fifties and handed them to him. "That's better, now in the back, move!"

Ten minutes later, the old woman was tied up and gagged in the back of the store. Al was walking down the street as if nothing had happened. Twenty minutes after that, a customer found the old woman and called the police.

Al was long gone.

Detective Cooper was at his desk when the call came in. One of the other detectives recognized St. James on the surveillance video and called him. Now, he was in the back of the store reviewing the video with the other detective. "Is that him?" the man asked.

Cooper watched as the image on the screen struck the old woman in the face with the gun. "Yeah, that's him, and that looks like the officer's gun he stole when he shot her."

Mike was cleaning up the kitchen when the phone rang. "I'll get it," said Mikey. "Hello? Just a minute."

He looked at Kitty, "It's for you."

Kitty took the phone, "Hello?"

"Kitty?" a woman's voice asked. "This is Sandy Boyd, remember me?"

"Oh yes, Dr. Boyd's wife, from the ICU at City General, isn't it?"

"Yes," she replied. "Listen, Ronnie asked me to call you and tell you that your surgery is set for Sunday morning at 6 AM at Mercy. Is that okay?"

Kitty was stunned. "So soon! Hold on, let me check," she said. She covered the phone and told Mike. "The surgery is scheduled for Sunday morning, can you take me?"

"Of course," he said.

She uncovered the phone, "Yes, that will be fine. What time should I be there?"

"Try to be there about an hour early. That way you can be admitted and get through the Pre-Op stuff in plenty of time for surgery. Remember, nothing to eat or drink after midnight Saturday, okay?"

"Yeah, no problem," Kitty replied.

"Okay then, I'll see you Sunday," Sandy said.

"You're going to be there? I thought you worked at City General," Kitty blurted out, confused.

"I do," Sandy replied. "But when Ronnie does cases like this, I help him. It's the only time we get to work together."

Sunday morning everyone got up at 4 AM. Mike and the boys didn't eat or drink anything because they didn't want Kitty to feel uncomfortable as they ate. They needn't have worried. She couldn't have eaten anything even if she wanted to. There wasn't any room in her stomach for food; it was too full of butterflies.

They rode to the hospital in silence. The main entrance was not open at that time in the morning so they had to go through the Emergency Room entrance. They checked in at the desk, and Kitty was taken into a small room to fill out the paperwork for admittance. When she came out, she saw all three of them were still there.

"You guys don't have to stay you know. I can call you when I wake up after it's over and let you know how it went," she told them.

"Don't be ridiculous," Mike said, "We're not going anywhere until we know you're okay."

The boys nodded their heads in agreement with their dad.

The four of them sat together not saying anything. About twenty minutes later, they heard someone walking toward them. They all looked up and saw a nurse coming down the hall. Kitty recognized Sandy Boyd immediately. She stopped in front of group and smiled, "Don't look like you're going to a funeral. This should be a hopeful moment. Kitty, if you're ready, I'll take you back to Pre-Op."

Kitty was too nervous to speak so she just nodded.

Sandy unlocked the wheels of her wheelchair. Turning to go, she said to Mike, "You guys can go get something to eat if you want. The operation is going to take several hours. In fact, if you want, you can go home, and I'll call you when it's over."

Mike replied, "No, we're not going anywhere. We'll be right here until she wakes up, and we find out how it went."

"Well, then you can come with me. I'll take you to the Operating Room waiting area. It's a little more comfortable than here," Sandy motioned and they all got up to followed her.

Just before Sandy wheeled Kitty into the Pre-Op area, they wished her good luck. As Kitty was being prepped for the operation, Mike and the boys went to the cafeteria, one at a time, then settled in for a long wait.

The operation took most of the day. While they waited, Mike and the boys watched two baseball games. As the third game was about to begin, Sandy came walking through the double doors at the end of the hall.

Once again they all looked up as she approached. She smiled, "Well, it was a lot harder than Ronnie expected. There was more damage which meant his team had to go slower than normal, but we think everything is going to be okay." She continued, "Kitty's in Recovery right now. She should be waking up in a few minutes. If you'd like, I can take you there."

They nodded and got up. Together they followed Sandy down the hall and into the recovery rooms. Kitty was still unconscious when they gathered around her bed. Mike looked around at all the monitors, tubes and IVs attached to her. *'She looks so small and helpless lying there,* he thought to himself. This scene was all too familiar from her assault and it sent a shiver of fear through him again.

Kitty opened her eyes and saw Mike and his sons smiling down at her. Groggily she said, "I guess I'm still alive then. Have you seen the doctor? Did he say how it went?"

Mike took her hand, "Yes, you're still alive. No, we haven't seen the doctor, but we did talk to Sandy. She said the operation was more difficult than they expected but everything went well and you should be okay." Then he asked, "How do you feel?"

"I don't know yet. My mouth is dry as dust, but other than that, I guess I'm alright."

Just then a nurse came over and saw Kitty was awake. She checked her vital signs, smiled at her, and announced, "Dr. Boyd will be in to see you in a few minutes. Then, we'll take you to your room. Are you feeling any pain?"

"No, just a little dizzy."

"Well, that's to be expected. It'll wear off in a little while." Then, as she turned to leave she said, "Call me if you're experiencing any pain or if you need anything. I'm going to let Dr. Boyd know you're awake."

Al counted the money. *Not bad,* he thought, fo*ur hundred and fifty-seven dollars. Not a bad morning's work.* He put the money into his front jeans pocket and continued walking. About a half hour later, he walked into a corner diner and ordered the first good meal he'd had in days.

Kitty's room was on the fifth floor. She shared the room with a middle aged woman waiting for heart bypass surgery scheduled the next day. She seemed cheerful and reminded Kitty of her aunt. Her side of the room was filled with flowers and balloons and she always had a smile on her face.

The day after the surgery, Dr. Boyd came in to see her. Kitty was sitting up in her bed and Chris was with her. Mike was at work, and Mikey was back at the apartment at the pool. As he strode into the room, Dr. Boyd asked, "How's my favorite patient today?"

Kitty smiled back at him, "Pretty good, I think. Have you got any good news for me?"

Dr. Boyd smiled as he pulled the covers off Kitty's feet, "I don't know, let's see what your feet tell us."

He picked up her left foot and scraped his pen along the bottom of it. Kitty jerked her foot and Dr. Boyd smiled. Then he picked up her right foot and did the same test. She jerked slightly and Dr. Boyd frowned.

"What's the matter?" she asked when she saw his face.

"Oh, it's nothing. It's just your right leg doesn't respond as well as your left leg. Hopefully, all that means is the nerves are healing slower than the other leg. We'll just have to wait a few days and see if it gets better. It should so don't worry about it. In the meantime, are you ready to begin your physical therapy? The sooner we get you on your feet the sooner you can get out of here."

She nodded.

"Great, I'll call therapy and get you started today. Well, I guess that's about it for now, I'll see you tomorrow."

She watched him walk out. Turning, she looked at Chris, "What if my right leg never gets better? Do you think I'll be able to walk on it, and, if I can, do you think I'll have a limp?"

Chris didn't have the slightest idea, but he thought he'd better sound optimistic in any case. "I'm sure it's like he said, the nerves aren't returning to normal as fast as the ones for the left leg are. We'll just have to wait and see how it goes. I'll bet they'll both be as good as new in a few days, just relax and see what happens."

An hour later, Kitty had her first physical therapy session. When she came back to the room, she knew it would be more than a few days for things to get back to normal.

CHAPTER 11

The robbery of the corner store wasn't the top story on the news that night, but it was in the first ten minutes. The local television stations had agreed to show Al's picture and ask the public for help finding him. When he saw it, Al knew he'd better get out of town fast. He decided to check out the bus station again, to see if the cops were still hanging out looking for him. He didn't even have to go inside. Two police cars were parked in front.

Kitty's parents hired a private investigator to search for her when she ran away. Although he kept telling them he was following up on leads, he didn't have any. After months of fruitless searching, he decided to tell them he wasn't having any luck. He liked the money they were paying him, but he was beginning to feel guilty taking it. Something would have to break soon if he was to stay on their payroll.

Chills ran up and down Kitty's spine when she saw Al's picture plastered all over the news. When she heard all that he was wanted for, she felt she was lucky to still be alive. She tried to keep her reaction to seeing Al on TV from showing on her face, but it didn't work. Mike saw her expression change and gently squeezed her hand as the story ran.

Therapy was starting to pay off. Kitty could stand and walk for about half an hour now, and she was ready to go home. *Home. Did she mean the apartment she shared with Mike or her real home where she had servants to do everything for her?* Even after everything she'd been through she realized she'd rather live in that cramped little apartment with Mike than to go to a gilded prison.

Al was tired of sleeping in alleys and smelling like a trash pile. He wanted a bed with clean sheets and a hot shower. He felt one night in a soft bed would be worth the risk. He counted his remaining money and found he had about a hundred bucks left. That meant he'd have to get a room in a sleaze-bag motel. Somewhere the clerks didn't ask too many questions.

It was around midnight when Al walked into the Roach Motel. The lighting was dim, and he had to ring the bell four times before a sleepy desk clerk finally stumbled out of the back room. "Yeah, what can I do for you?"

"I'd like a room for the night," Al answered. He'd pulled his cap low and kept his head down, hoping the clerk wouldn't recognize him.

The clerk said automatically, "Just the one night? You'll have to pay in advance then. That'll be $37.80, including tax. Check out's at noon."

Al pulled money out of his front pocket, peeled off two twenties, and handed them to the clerk.

As he took the money, the clerk glanced at his face but Al didn't notice. The clerk's heart began racing as he recognized him. With his hand shaking slightly he handed Al a key and his change, "Room 15, right around the corner on the left."

Al took the key and the money, mumbled, "Thanks," and walked away.

The clerk stared at his back as he left. As soon as Al rounded the corner, the clerk dashed into the back room and picked up the phone.

When Kitty checked out of the hospital on Saturday, Mike and the boys were waiting for her. She was wheeled out of the front door, much to her chagrin. After months of having to be in a wheelchair, she hated the sight of the thing. As they went out the doors, TV cameras and photographers crowded around.

"What's all this about?" Kitty asked.

"Oh, some actor was in for exhaustion and is being released today. They should be coming out soon," replied the nurse.

Just then the actor's entourage came out the door behind them. The cameras swung around and started filming, catching Kitty and her friends in their lenses. Kitty lowered her head, "Come on, let's get out of here. I don't like cameras."

When they got back to the apartment, she was in for a shock. As soon as Kitty opened the door and turned on the lights. Michelle, Sandy, and Dr. Boyd stood up and yelled, "Surprise!" She jumped but grinned as they crowded around her.

Michelle handed her a glass of champagne, "I know technically, if you drink that, I should arrest you, but just this once, I'll make an exception."

Everyone laughed, and Mike added, "You'd have to arrest me too for letting Mikey and Chris drink."

Kitty looked around and saw balloons and a huge banner that read "Welcome Home!" greeting her hung above the patio door. She looked on the table and saw a huge cake with the words, "Welcome Home Kitty" on it. Tears of happiness filled her eyes. She hugged each of them and said, "Thank you. You don't know how much this means to me."

The party lasted until almost midnight. Ronnie ordered pizza and everyone had a huge piece of cake, and, of course, more champagne. All too soon, it was time for people to leave. Michelle left first, saying she had to get some sleep because she had to work in the morning.

Then, Sandy and Ronnie left. As he was saying good-bye, he told Kitty, "I think it's time for you to go to bed too, young lady. You've had a busy day, and I don't want you to overdo." As he hugged her he said, "Take it easy for the next few days okay? You were stuck in that wheelchair for months and it'll take more than a few days to get your strength back."

Kitty tried to helped Mike and the boys clean up, but they shooed her away. She kissed them all and said thank you more times than she could remember. They all told her it was nothing and were all happy the surgery had gone so well. When she crawled into bed a few minutes later, she felt a happy glow she hadn't felt in a very long time. She stretched out luxuriously and fell asleep in a few minutes.

Al decided to take two showers, one with his clothes on and one with his clothes off. *What sense was there in taking a shower and getting all clean and then put on dirty clothes*, he asked himself? *None*, he reasoned, *And since I don't have any clean clothes why not wash the clothes I'm wearing while I take a shower?*

After his second shower, he hung up his wet clothes and walked back into the bedroom. He turned on the TV and poured himself a drink. After his third drink, he crawled under the covers and fell instantly asleep.

The phone rang two times when the clerk heard, "9-1-1 please state the nature of your emergency."

"Ah, yeah, I don't know how to explain," he began. "I was watching the news tonight and they showed a picture of this guy that's wanted for a bunch of stuff. Well, anyway, I think he just checked into my motel."

"What's the address, sir?"

Al was having the nicest dream he'd had in weeks when the motel door burst open. Before he could blink twice, he was thrown from the bed onto the floor and handcuffed. After a quick search of the room, the cops found the gun and what was left of the cash he'd stolen in the robbery.

The cops were nice enough to help him put on his wet pants before they dragged him out of the motel room. As he walked out the door, TV camera lights blinded him. Some reporter yelled questions at him. As he was dragged to the waiting police car, he called out, "I didn't do nothin'! They got the wrong guy!"

The phone rang at seven the morning after the party. Kitty heard Mike say, "Hello? Just a minute," he covered the phone and yelled, "Kitty, Detective Cooper's on the phone. He says they caught the guy who attacked you. He wants to know if you'd come down to identify the guy."

Kitty was instantly awake. With her heart racing she hollered, "Yeah, when does he want me to come down?"

There was a pause while Mike relayed the question and then he called out, "He wants to know if nine o'clock is too early. He says he'll send someone to pick you up if that's okay."

Kitty got out of bed and put her bathrobe on. As she walked out of the bedroom, she said, "I'll be ready and waiting."

Al was sitting alone in a holding cell at police headquarters. *What's going on*, he wondered? *Nobody's asked me a single question; they just read me my rights and stuck me in here. No phone call, no lawyer, nothing but silence and cold.* They hadn't even given him dry clothes to put on.

An hour later, a cop came over and unlocked his cell. "Come with me St. James, Detective Cooper wants a word with you."

The officer placed handcuffs on him and led him to an interview room. He sat down on a well-worn plastic chair across a Formica covered battered table from Detective Cooper. As he sat, Al said, "I ain't sayin' nothin' till I see a lawyer."

"That's fine," Cooper replied. "Do you have a lawyer or do you want one from the Public Defender's Office?"

"Man, if I had any money, do you think I'd have held up that little grocery store? I need a public defender."

Cooper got up and went out the door. He came back a moment later, followed by a skinny bald man in a crumpled suit.

Al thought the guy looked like he'd slept in his suit for a week.

Cooper looked down at Al, "I figured you'd want a public defender so I had Mr. Hopkins waiting in my office. I'll give you two some time to talk and then I'll be back."

After Cooper left, the lawyer sat down and began asking questions. An hour later, Cooper returned. "Well, now that you've had a chance to talk to an attorney are you ready to answer some questions?"

"No," Al said.

When the knock came on the door, Kitty answered it. "Michelle!" she cried, "I didn't think they'd send you!"

Michelle smiled, "When they called for someone to come over and pick you up, I just couldn't resist. I had to take the run." Then she asked, "Well, are you ready?"

Kitty replied, "Yeah, just let me grab my purse and cane, then I'll be ready."

When the two friends walked into the line-up viewing room, Detective Cooper was waiting for them. "Miss Benson, we'd like you to look through the glass and see if you recognize the man who instigated the attack on you."

Kitty's heart was pounding in her chest as she looked through the two-way mirror. It only took her a second to recognize Al. "That's him," she said in a shaky voice. "Number six. That's the guy."

"Are you sure?" Cooper asked.

"Yeah, I'm sure. That's the guy who grabbed me and slammed me into the wall." She looked at Cooper, "Can I go now? I don't want to be anywhere near that creep."

As Michelle took Kitty home, Cooper met with Assistant District Attorney Greene and laid out his case. After listening to all the evidence, she agreed to process all the charges. "If we get convictions on all counts," the attorney said, "this guy will be put away forever, good job. Once he's indicted, I'll meet with his attorney and see what he's willing to plea to. Maybe we can put him away without a lengthy trial."

Three days later, the grand jury indictment came down on all counts.

CHAPTER 12

The 'In Town' Show was on after the news on Sunday night. Kitty's stomach fell to her feet as she watched herself coming out of the hospital just before the famous actor came out. The announcer was talking about the actor, but she wasn't paying attention to what he said. Instead, she watched in horror as the cameras closed in on her for a second or two before they panned to the actor behind her. She prayed nobody who knew her watched the program and recognized her. Her prayer would not be answered.

He was bored and couldn't sleep. The TV was on and some stupid celebrity chasing show was on. As he finished his last beer, he watched the images on the screen. When he saw Kitty, he almost choked on his beer. There she was, coming out of a hospital with three guys he didn't know. He picked up the phone and hit the speed dial.

Mike was in his office reviewing a client's file when his phone rang. "This is Mike Hatfield, how may I help you?"

"Mike," his ex-wife said, "Did you know you and the boys were on TV last night?"

"What are you talking about?" he asked, slightly confused.

"I was watching the 'In Town' TV show last night. They were doing a story about Allen Smithson leaving the hospital. I saw you three with that girl you live with coming out of the hospital in front of him. When I saw you guys, I couldn't believe it. You guys are TV stars! How does it feel to be famous?" Sharron joked.

He walked into the TV production company and approached the receptionist. "Can I help you?" she asked as he stopped in front of her desk.

"Yes, my name is William Long, and I'm here to see Clarence Newberg."

"Oh, yes. Please have a seat, and I'll let Mr. Newberg know you're here."

It only took five minutes before he was ushered into Newberg's office. As he entered, the man behind the desk rose and offered his hand. "Mr. Long, I'm Clarence Newberg. Mr. Burgess called me this morning and asked if I'd see you. What can I do for you?"

He took the offered hand and shook it. As the man sat back down, he said, "Mr. Newberg, I'm a private investigator. I represent a family whose teenage daughter ran away from home a few months back." After a brief pause he went on, "I was watching one of your programs last night when I saw a story about an actor leaving a hospital. Do you know the story I mean?"

"Yes, that was Allen Smithson leaving Mercy Hospital after being treated for exhaustion." He scoffed, "Exhaustion my foot. More like detox after a drinking binge."

"Yes, that's the story I'm talking about. At the beginning of the story the camera focused on a young woman in a wheelchair before it panned to the actor. Do you know who that woman was?"

"No, I have no idea. I guess she was being released at the same time. Why?"

"I think she might be the girl I'm looking for," Long replied.

Newberg picked up the phone. After a second he said, "Leslie, could you bring me the Smithson report from last night please."

Newberg could smell a story. He asked, "So, who's this girl?"

"She's the runaway daughter of a very important businessman," he answered.

"Really, what's her name?"

Long smiled, "Mr. Newberg, you know I can't reveal that information. It would be a violation of professional ethics. But I will tell you this; if this got out, it would be front page news."

They watched the footage and Long pointed out the close-up of Kitty. "Can I get a still of her?"

"Of course," Newberg called his secretary again. Ten minutes later,

Long was in his car heading for Mercy Hospital.

Meanwhile, Newberg told his secretary, "Find out who this girl is and what she was doing at the hospital."

Kitty didn't say anything about being on TV to anyone. Instead, she acted as if she hadn't seen the story and went about her day as usual. Since the operation she went to the apartment complex's gym for an hour every day. She walked on the treadmill and used weight machines to strengthen her legs. Then, she would go to the pool with Mikey and Chris. The first time they went, Kitty joked, "With all these scars, I guess my bikini days are over."

Chris replied, "One piece or two, you look good in a bathing suit to me."

She blushed and playfully punched him in the shoulder as she grabbed her cane.

It took almost three days before Long's informant came through. He found out the girl was a charity case by the name of Kitty Benson. She'd been raped and severely beaten months ago and needed surgery to restore the use of her legs. His clients were not going to be happy.

Newberg paid a fortune for the information, but now he had the story of the year. Mega-industrialist Brian Madison's sixteen year-old daughter had run away, been raped and beaten, and was now living with a middle-aged divorced man in an apartment in midtown. This was explosive stuff, but he had to be careful how he reported it.

Kitty was getting stronger. She still needed to use a cane. She will need a cane for the rest of her life, but her last trip to the mall didn't wear her out like it had before. Now, she and Chris were going dancing, and she hoped her legs could keep up.

Mike was sitting up waiting for Chris and Kitty to come home. The TV was on and 'In Town' came on. The announcer exclaimed "Tonight, on 'In Town' what was the heiress of a mega-industrialist doing coming out of a local hospital with these men?"

Mike looked up and his jaw dropped. He watched Kitty being wheeled out of the hospital with him and the boys beside her. *Who was the announcer talking about? It couldn't be Kitty. She wasn't an heiress, was she?* After a couple commercials the program came back on.

Mike turned up the volume as a woman reporter said, "Bruce, 'In Town' has learned that Kathleen Madison, the daughter of mega-industrialist Brian Madison, has been missing for several months. The sixteen year-old was recently seen coming out of Mercy Hospital in the company of three unknown men. Sources have confirmed Miss Madison is going under an assumed name and recently underwent spinal surgery to repair a serious injury that left her paralyzed from the chest down. An informer who wished to remain anonymous revealed Miss Madison was brutally beaten and assaulted earlier this year and has been living with this unidentified man."

The screen showed a close-up of Mike's face. The reporter went on, "A family spokesman refused to comment on Miss Madison's whereabouts and a spokesman for the Metropolitan police stated they had no information about Miss Madison's disappearance or any criminal cases involving her. 'In Town" will continue to follow this story."

Mike turned off the TV and stared at the blank screen. The telephone rang and startled him out of his thoughts. "Hello?"

"Mike, what the hell's going on?" Sharron's voice said, "Why didn't you tell me that girl was Kathleen Madison? And what are you doing dragging our kids into this? Did you know she was underage? Do you realize you could go to jail for living with her?"

"Sharron, I swear I didn't know that was her name. She told me her name was Kitty Benson. She said she was eighteen! She even told the detective the same thing. I don't know what else to say," he replied.

"Where's Chris and Mikey?' Sharron demanded. "I want them out of there this instant! If you want to get yourself arrested for harboring a runaway underage rich girl that's your business, but you're not getting my kids arrested!"

"Mikey's gone to the movies, and Chris is out with Kitty. I think they went dancing or something. I'm not going to be arrested. Honestly, Sharron, what would they arrest me for, being nice to a poor beat up young girl who lied to me? Be reasonable. And as for sending the boys home, I'll talk to them when they get in, and let you know what we're doing tomorrow. That's the best I can do."

"You're an idiot, Mike!" Sharron bellowed, "Have you ever heard of Statutory Rape? How about child abuse, and oh, I don't know, but you can bet that girl's parents have got lawyers working on charging you with something, that's for sure. I'll expect your phone call telling me the boys are on their way home tomorrow morning," and with that, she hung up the phone.

Mike put the phone back in its cradle and stared at it blankly. *Was he about to be arrested?*

Kitty was having a wonderful evening. She loved the music and even braved the dance floor for a couple of slow dances. Chris was a perfect gentleman all evening, but it was getting late and she was getting tired. "Chris," she shouted in his ear over the blaring music, "Can we go home now? I'm getting a little tired."

He nodded and helped her get up. As they walked out through the front door, they were met by at least a dozen photographers. Momentarily blinded by the strobes going off in their faces, Kitty stumbled.

Chris caught her, and she threw her arms around his neck to steady herself. The cameras went crazy! As he helped her to stand up again, the reporters were calling, "Miss Madison, over here!"

"Why did you run away from home, Miss Madison?"

"Who's your boyfriend?"

Kitty grabbed Chris' hand, "Let's get out of here."

As they hurried to Chris's car he asked, "Who's Miss Madison? Kitty, what's going on?"

"Just get in," she said, "I'll explain later."

They sped off as quickly as they could. As they turned a corner, Chris asked, "What's that about?"

Kitty didn't answer right away. She just stared out the window.

"Kitty, what's going on?" Chris asked her again. "I thought your name was Benson, not Madison."

Kitty sighed and looked over at him, "I lied. I'm not Kitty Benson. My real name is Kathleen Madison, and I'm not eighteen, I'm sixteen. About a year ago, a friend helped me get a fake ID to get into the clubs. " She drew in a deep breath before continuing, "I ran away from home several months ago because I couldn't stand living with my straight-laced parents anymore. When I got here, I spent several days on the streets. Then I met your dad by the diner, and well, you know what happened after that."

When Chris didn't say anything she looked back out the window.

Softly, she added, "I'm sorry, Chris."

They rode the rest of the way home in silence, each deep in their own thoughts. Chris didn't see the car following them three cars back.

Long had seen the report on 'In Town' and knew he was out of time. He picked up the phone and called his clients, they weren't going to be happy, he thought as the phone rang. He was right.

"What kind of a private detective are you," Mr. Madison demanded. "You're getting paid to find our daughter discreetly, not plaster her picture all over the television!"

"I'm sorry, Mr. Madison. I had nothing to do with that," he replied.

"I should hope not," Mr. Madison demanded, calming down a little. "Did you at least find out where she's living, and who those men are in the pictures?"

"Yes, I have that information. I'll send it to your email account."

"No, never mind about that, just meet us at the Crown Royale Hotel tomorrow at noon. We're coming to get our daughter, and you'd better be able to take us to her." The line went dead.

"Kitty, why didn't you tell me who you really were instead of lying to me? I thought we were friends," Mike accused as she walked through the door.

"I thought you'd turn me in if you knew who I really was," she replied.

"It's been all over the TV," Mike said. "Your mother called and wants you two to go home right away," he said looking at Chris and Mikey.

They both began to protest, but Mike held up his hand to stop them. "I think she's right," he said. "The odds are once Kitty's parents find out about me, they'll have me arrested. I don't want you two around if and when that happens. Tomorrow morning, I want you both to pack up and go back to your grandparents' place. No arguments."

The phone rang and Mike picked it up. "Hello?" he answered. After a moment he said, "No, there's nobody here by that name." He hung up the phone. A second later the phone rang again, and the same pattern was repeated.

The fourth time the phone rang, Mike ignored it. He looked at Kitty, "I think you'd better pack your things too. Tomorrow, I'll take you home. Hopefully, everything will be okay. I'll speak to your parents and explain everything. Maybe they won't have me arrested. Now, I think we all need to go to bed. Maybe things will look better in the light of day. Maybe, but I doubt it."

Kitty hung her head in shame and went to her room.

CHAPTER 13

The phone didn't stop ringing all night. Finally, in an effort to gain some peace and quiet, and maybe a little sleep, Mike took it off the hook and threw it in a drawer. It didn't help, he didn't sleep.

Kitty didn't sleep either, she lay in bed with tears streaming down her cheeks staring at the ceiling. In the morning, she'd have to go home and face her parents. Mike was right. They'd probably have him arrested if they could. She'd have to do something to keep that from happening. She rolled over on her side and pummeled her pillow.

Bill Long was waiting when the Madisons walked into the hotel's lobby. He walked toward them, hand extended to Mr. Madison. He didn't take it but just kept walking to the front desk.

After checking in, they went directly to their room. They never acknowledged Long or spoke to him until after the porter put their luggage in the bedroom and left. Mr. Madison motioned for Long to follow him and sat in the living room area of the hotel suite. "Now, Mr. Long, where's my daughter?"

Bill consulted his notebook, "She's living with a man named Michael Hatfield, a recently divorced thirty-nine year-old with two teenage sons who are presently visiting him. They live at 2325 West Pickett Street, Apartment 1C." He looked up from his notes, "I can take you there, if you'd like."

As they drove, Mrs. Madison asked, "The TV reporter said something about Kitty being beaten and assaulted. What happened?"

Long replied, "Not long after she came to town, she was brutally beaten and gang raped. She spent almost a month in the hospital and was paralyzed from the chest down until about a month ago when she had spinal surgery. I checked with my contacts in the police department. They have no record of Kitty Madison being assaulted, but they do have a report of a Kitty Benson being assaulted. Kitty Benson matches your daughter's description to a tee."

"So," Mr. Madison asked, "Where's this Michael Hatfield fit into all this?"

"I haven't been able to find out about that. My police contact told me your daughter was found at the crime scene with his name and number in her pocket along with identification in the name of Kathleen Benson who was allegedly eighteen. Apparently, he took her home with him when she was discharged from the hospital," Long told the Madisons as they pulled into the apartment complex parking lot.

"No Mom, Mikey and I don't want to come home right now. We still have three weeks before Mikey goes back to school, and we want to spend them with Dad," Chris told his mother on the phone.

"I really don't care what you want Christopher. I want the both of you out of there today! So pack your bags, get in your car, and come home immediately! Immediately mister, do you hear me?"

"No, Mom. We're not going back to Grandma's. We hate it there. We're staying here until school starts. Now, I've got to go, there's someone at the door, and Dad's in the shower."

He hung up the phone and answered the door. He was surprised when he saw three adults he didn't recognize.

"Good morning, is Mr. Michael Hatfield in? We'd like to speak to him," Long said.

Before Chris could answer, the other man pushed him aside and walked into the apartment. "I don't care about him. Where's my daughter?"

Madison looked around and when he didn't see her, he bellowed, "Kitty! Come out here right now!"

Kitty walked out of the bedroom and found her parents staring at her. "Hi, Daddy," was all she could think to say.

"Ten months, and all I get is 'hi Daddy'?" he roared. "Do you have any idea what your mother and I have been going through since you took off?"

Kitty didn't say anything. She simply walked past them and sat down at the table. Everyone stared at her, waiting for her to respond. Normally, she would scream back at her father but not today. She wasn't going to lose her temper in front of all these people.

"I'm perfectly aware of what you went through. You spent a lot of money keeping my disappearance out of the newspapers, and even more on private detectives to find me and drag me back to that hell-hole you jokingly call a home." She looked at her father and continued, "It's not that you care one iota about me leaving, you were only concerned about how it would look to your friends and business associates if your only child was so miserable at home she preferred living on the streets to living with you. Isn't that right, Daddy. All you care about is you and your reputation. I know it, so don't try to play the concerned parent role. It doesn't fit."

"Kathleen," her mother said, "that's not true, and it's not fair either. We love you, and we were worried sick about you. Why would you say such things?"

"I say them because they're true, Mother," Kitty replied bitterly.

"Enough of this," her father railed, "Get your things. You're coming home with us."

"No, I'm not," Kitty asserted. "I'm staying right here. I've finally found people who care about me because of me, not just because of who you are. Me! Kitty Benson. A completely different and distinct individual from Brian and Carolyn Madison and all their money and power. But, that's something you probably will never understand."

"Whether I understand or not is irrelevant. You're still underage and you really have nothing to say about it until you're eighteen. Now, get your stuff and let's go."

"No." The word was firm and unmoving.

"You know, we can force you to come home with us," her father declared. "And if you resist, I'll have your friend arrested. Then, you'll have nowhere to go but home."

Kitty stood and glared at her father. "If you have Mike arrested," she hissed, "I'll make your life a living hell. I'll tell everyone about your dirty little secrets, and your shady business dealings, and the crooked characters that come calling all hours of the day and night. Then, you'll be sorry."

Her father laughed a mirthless laugh. "Don't try and threaten me, little girl. You'll be biting off more than you can chew. You're still my daughter, and if you sully my reputation, you'll only be hurting yourself. Who do you think pays for your fancy private schools, all your nice little parties, and the pretty little dresses you buy almost every week? Who do you think buys you out of trouble every time you throw a little temper tantrum and destroy someone's house? Me that's who! Don't make threats you can't keep."

"Get out!" she roared "Get out and leave me alone!"

Carolyn could see a major fight elevating and decided this was neither the time nor the place. She took Brian by the arm and began pulling him away. As they headed for the door, her father looked at her, "We'll be back to pick you up in an hour, and we'll bring the police with us to arrest your lover."

Kitty sat back down and buried her face in her hands as the door slammed. Chris sat down beside her and put his arm around her. She turned and buried her head in his chest, her shoulders shaking with sobs.

"Brian, don't be ridiculous," Carolyn snapped as they drove back to the hotel. "If we try to force Kitty to come home, she'll just run away again."

"Well, what do you want me to do," he goaded. "Give her a pat on the head and let her go on treating us like trash? No, this time she's gone too far. I'm not going to put up with her antics anymore. No, she's coming home and staying there if I have to lock her in her room till she's twenty-one. I've had it!"

"Brian, let's go back to the hotel and try to think this through a little. We can have Mr. Long tail her until we decide what to do. Maybe, when the two of you calm down, we can come to some sort of a compromise." She patted his leg, "In the meantime, let me try something."

"Like what?"

She smiled, "Oh, I've got something in mind that might help."

For the rest of the ride back to the hotel, Carolyn refused to tell him her plan.

Al was sitting in the interview room with his forehead in his hands as his lawyer paced back and forth. "I met with Jennifer Greene from the District Attorney's Office and saw the evidence they have against you. Not to put too fine a point on it, you're screwed nine ways to Sunday," he told him. "They've got surveillance tape of you beating and robbing that old woman in the market, they've got dash-cam footage of you struggling with the cop and shooting her, shooting the other guy and steeling the car, and they've got witnesses and DNA evidence from the rape and beating of that girl."

Al shrugged.

His attorney paused and added, "And speaking of that girl, do you know who she is? She's the daughter of one of the most powerful men in the country. On top of that, she's only sixteen so the charges were changed to First Degree Sex Abuse of a Minor. Child rape. Buddy, when you screw up, you really screw up."

Al finally looked frightened. Looking at his attorney, he asked, "So what do think I should do?"

"The DA is willing to let you plea to shooting of the cop, the armed carjacking, and the robbery charges. She's offering fifty to seventy-five years with the possibility of parole after forty. If I were you I'd jump at it. If the case goes to trial you will end up with forty years just for the rape and beating of that girl, let alone all the rest of the charges your facing. You're seriously looking at life without parole all charges together. You know, I've been a public defender for over thirty years and don't think I've ever had a client as screwed as you are."

"I guess, I don't really have a choice, do I?"

"It's up to you, but if you take my advice, take the plea deal and hope for the best."

"Alright," he said, "Tell them I'll take it."

The lawyer sighed and said, "I'll tell the DA and see you at the Preliminary Hearing."

Mike was at his desk, working on a proposal on his computer when there was a knock on the door. "Come in," he called and turned toward the door.

"Mike, the boss wants to see you," said his coworker.

Mike looked confused. "Why didn't Amanda just call me if she wanted to see me?" he asked.

"It's not Amanda who wants to see you. It's the big boss. Come on, I'll take you there."

He got up and followed the man down the hall, eventually ending up at the executive conference room. As they turned the corner, Mike saw two men in suits standing on each side of the doors to the conference room. As he approached, one of the men silently opened the door. Mike walked in totally befuddled.

As the door closed behind him, he saw the back of a woman sitting at the far end of the conference table. He stopped just inside the door and said, "You wanted to see me?"

When the woman turned around Mike's jaw dropped. Even though he had been in the shower when Kitty's parents visited, he knew who was looking at him from across the table. She looked like an older version of her daughter. "You're the big boss?" he asked, incredulously.

She smiled up at him, "Madison Industries owns eighty percent of this company. I represent Madison Industries on the Board of Directors, so, yes, I'm the big boss."

As he stared blankly at Carolyn Madison she added, "Please sit down Mr. Hatfield."

After he complied with her request, she smiled at him, "Don't look at me as if I'm going to have you executed. Rest assured, I only want to talk to you to get to know you a little better. Would you like some coffee?"

He nodded. She poured him a cup. "Cream or sugar?" she asked.

"No thank you, just black," he replied finally getting his voice back.

She handed him the coffee, "Mr. Hatfield, I want to talk to you about Kitty." As he began to protest she added, "I don't believe you and her are lovers, if that's what you think this is all about. No, I wanted to ask you about how you met her and ended up living with her."

"How did you find out I work here?" he inquired.

She laughed, "We're having you and Kitty both followed. How else are we going to find out what's going on? She really seems to like your oldest son, by the way."

Mike felt his face growing hot as he looked at Carolyn. "I'm not sure I'm the one you should be talking to about this. Shouldn't you be asking your daughter? And as far as my son is concerned, how do you know Kitty likes him? Are you having him tailed too?"

Again, she laughed. "Oh, we don't need to do that. It was on that TV show, 'In Town,' last night. Imagine how surprised we were to see our daughter walking out of a dance club with your son, especially since she's only sixteen. Now, can we get back to your relationship with Kitty?"

And so, he told her how they met and how she came to live with him. When he finished, she asked, "Is that why you ended up divorced, because of Kitty?"

"No," Mike said honestly. "My divorce came about because of financial and personal problems, not because of Kitty. My wife said she found another man she liked better. With all due respect, I don't think my divorce is any of your business anyway," he added.

"No, of course not," she reassured.

"So, now that I've answered your questions, let me ask you one. What made her run away?" Mike asked.

"That's a long story," Carolyn sighed. "Let's just say her vision of her future does not match her father's. Add to that she's sort of a free spirit and he's very straitlaced, and I'm sure you can see why they don't get along." She stood up, "Now, perhaps you'll accompany me back to your apartment? I'd like to talk to my daughter, and I think you should be there too."

He stood up and shook her offered hand. As she walked him to the door, she added, "And don't worry about being arrested, my husband didn't really mean it. He hates publicity, especially when it comes to the family."

CHAPTER 14

Detective Cooper was sitting in the courtroom, directly behind the prosecutor's table. The bailiff called out, "All rise!"

When the judge sat down behind the bench, he stated, "Be seated." Once everyone sat back down, the judge continued, "Bailiff, call the first case."

"The People versus Alton St. James, Docket number 495397."

One of the bailiffs opened a door next to the Defendant's table, and Al was brought out in chains. He walked over and stood beside his attorney. The judge asked, "Is the prosecution ready?"

"We are, your honor," replied Assistant District Attorney Jennifer Greene.

"And is the defense ready?"

"We are," Al's lawyer responded.

"I have been advised the two parties have reached a plea agreement," the judge inquired, "Is that correct?"

"We have, your honor," replied the prosecutor. "The defendant has agreed to plead guilty to the Attempted Murder of a Police Officer, Armed Carjacking, and First Degree Assault, and First Degree Robbery with a weapon. The state has agreed to Nolle Proserui the remaining charges and recommend a sentence of fifty to seventy-five years with the possibility of parole after forty years," she concluded.

The judge looked at Al, "Mr. St. James, has your attorney explained this plea agreement to you?"

"Yeah," Al replied.

"And do you understand this agreement," the judge asked.

"Yeah."

"Has anyone promised you anything in exchange for agreeing to this plea agreement, other than the agreement itself?"

"Nope."

"And do you also understand by accepting your guilty plea, the Court is not bound by any sentencing agreement? The Court may decide to impose a stiffer sentence if, in its opinion, it would be in the best interest of the people to do so. Do you understand, Mr. St. James?"

"Yeah."

"Very well, the Court will accept your plea of guilty to the agreed charges. You are hereby remanded to the custody of the Department of Corrections, pending a sentencing hearing, which will be set for sixty days from today's date. The Office of Pretrial Services will conduct a presentencing investigation to be completed prior to the hearing," the judge declared, pounding his gavel.

Cooper sat through three more guilty pleas, the other men involved in the rape case. When it was over, he stepped out of the courtroom feeling a sense of relief and accomplishment. He smiled at the thought of all four men who had brutally beaten and raped Kitty going to prison for a very long time. If only all his cases ended so well. He took out his cell phone and called Michelle to give her the good news.

Kitty felt Chris's hand rubbing her back as she cried on his shoulder. How could things get so messed up just when they seemed to be getting back on track? She looked up at Chris, tears in her eyes. "I'm sorry Chris," was all she could think of to say.

"Sorry? For what? You didn't do anything that you need to be sorry for. Do you think you're the first girlfriend who's had a fight with her parents in front of me?" he asked with a chuckle.

Did she hear him right? Did he just call her his girlfriend? Before she could think long on the question, Chris leaned over and kissed her gently on the lips. As he was kissing her, she felt her fears and anxiety melt away. *He has really soft lips,* she thought to herself.

The moment was spoiled when the phone rang. Mikey got up off the couch and answered it. After saying hello and listening for a couple of seconds, he handed the phone to Kitty saying, "Here, it's for you."

She took the phone, "Hello?"

"Kitty, it's Michelle. Are you busy?"

She hesitated for a second, and Michelle went on, "I won't keep you. I just wanted to let you know the four guys who attacked you have plead guilty! Isn't that great?"

Kitty smiled feeling both the satisfaction of revenge and a sense of relief that the whole thing was now over. Well, as over as it would ever be.

"That's great, Michelle! When were the trials?"

"No trials. The preliminary hearings were today, and they all agreed to plea deals. The ring leader got a minimum of forty years and the others got twenty."

"Great!" Kitty exclaimed.

Michelle could tell something wasn't right so she asked, "Kitty, are you okay? You sound like there's something wrong."

Half-heartedly, Kitty answered, "No, not really. I'm fine."

Now Michelle knew there was something wrong. "You sound like you need to talk. I get off in an hour. Would you like to go and get some coffee or something? Then you can tell me what's going on."

Kitty thought about it for a couple of seconds, "Yeah, that'd be great. I'll see you then."

"Great," Michelle said cheerily, "I'll see you around four."

Kitty hung up the phone.

"Who was that?" Chris asked.

Kitty told both him and Mikey the news about Al and his friends.

Chris gave her a hug, "That's great, I'm sure you feel relieved that's over."

"I knew they'd get 'em, the police always do." Mikey chimed in.

"I'm going to call Dad and give him the good news. He'll probably want to go out tonight and celebrate." Chris said. A minute later he hung up the phone, "Dad's in a meeting and couldn't come to the phone." Then, after a few seconds, he announced, "I know, let's surprise him and have a celebration here when he gets home."

Just then the door opened and all three teenagers turned, mouths gaping as Mike and Carolyn entered.

Mike could tell something had happened, but he couldn't imagine what. "What are you three looking so happy about?" he asked.

When Kitty didn't answer, Chris blurted, "Kitty's cop friend, Michelle, just called. The four guys who had attacked her have all copped pleas and been found guilty. Isn't that great?"

Carolyn walked over to Kitty and gave her a hug. "I'm so glad that's over. You must be relieved not to have to testify."

Kitty hugged her back. All of a sudden she felt like a little girl again. Tears started flowing, and she couldn't stop them. "Oh, Mom," she cried.

Mike looked at the two boys and motioned them toward the door. Without a word all three of them walked out and left mother and daughter alone. An hour later, Michelle found Mike and the boys sitting on the front stoop of the apartment building.

Kitty couldn't stop crying. Gently, Carolyn led her over to the couch and they sat down together. Through her sobs, Kitty said, "Mom, how could I have screwed things up so badly? I didn't really want to hurt you and Daddy. It's just he makes me so mad sometimes, that I don't know what I'm doing. One minute, I was screaming my head off at him and the next I was walking around the city with nothing to do and nowhere to go. I was so scared I could barely breathe."

Her mother patted her arm gently, "Sometimes we say and do things we regret later. I'm sure you didn't mean the things you said to your father. I know he didn't mean what he said to you. When you ran away, he didn't eat or sleep for days. I know you'll find it hard to believe, but he didn't go to work for almost a week, he just paced the floor for hours. I finally convinced him to go back to work and allow the private investigators to do their job."

"You must hate me," Kitty sobbed.

"Of course we don't hate you! We love you and always will."

After a few minutes Kitty stated, "They hurt me. They hurt me real bad."

"Who hurt you, baby?"

"The men who attacked me. For the rest of my life, I'll have to use a cane. My right leg won't be as strong as it once was. Dr. Boyd said the nerves were permanently damaged." She paused before adding. "And I can never have a baby. I'll never be able to give you and Daddy any grandchildren."

"Honey, none of that matters to us. You're all that matters."

"I've been so stupid."

"Yes you have, but all that's over now. Now we have to fix what we can and learn to live with the rest. Your father and I are here for you, and it seems you've found a very good friend in Mike Hatfield. It was kind of him to take you in and help you. Why do you think he did it?"

"I don't know," Kitty said honestly.

Her mother hesitated, "I met with him today at his office. He told me how he met you, and everything that's happened since He seems like a very nice man. Someone up there was looking out for you when you two met. But enough about the past, let's talk about the future. What do you want to do now?"

Kitty thought for a moment. "I don't want to come home," she blurted out. "I love you and Daddy very much, but I just can't live the way Daddy wants me to. I know I've acted like a spoiled little rich girl in the past, but that's not who I am now. I've change."

Her mother laughed, "Of course you've changed, how could you not? But you're still only sixteen. You're too young to live on your own."

"I know that too," Kitty said.

Both women sat thinking. At last, Carolyn sighed, "Well, let's sleep on it and maybe something will come to us." Then she smiled, "In the meantime, I think we've got a celebration to plan. Why don't your father and I take you and your friends out tonight to celebrate the convictions? Would you like that? Do you think Mr. Hatfield and his sons would agree to come?"

Kitty frowned and her mother said, "Don't worry about your father. I'll talk to him and straighten him out about Mike." She stood up, "In the meantime, why don't you talk Mike and his sons into it. I'll call you later to work out the details."

Kitty stood and smiled. "Okay, I guess that'd be good."

"Great, it's settled then," Carolyn said, and the two of them walked out the door to look for Mike and the boys.

They found them on the stoop with Michelle. After Kitty introduced her mother to Michelle, Carolyn asked, "Why don't you come too? We'll have fun. I've got to go, you know how your father is. He'll have worn a hole in the carpet by the time I get back."

Kitty took Chris's hand, and they all walked back into the apartment. Once everyone had sat down, Michelle looked at Kitty, "So that was your mother?"

"Yeah."

"What was she talking about inviting me too?" Michelle asked.

"She wants us all to go out tonight and celebrate the end of the rape case," Kitty said.

"That sounds like fun. Where are we going?"

"I don't know. I'm sure Dad will want to go someplace private and secluded. That doesn't sound like much of a celebration to me."

"Well," Michelle said, trying to cheer her up, "If we're going out tonight, why don't we go get something new to wear?" She got up and held her hand out to Kitty. "Come on; I've got a 20% off coupon for Robertson's, and they usually have some good stuff that's not too expensive."

The two girls left the guys at the apartment and went shopping. Before she left, Kitty gave Chris another kiss. After they were gone, Mike gave Chris a curious look, and Chris smiled. Mike was just about to ask him what was going on when the doorbell rang.

Mike opened the door and his jaw dropped. Sharron was standing on the step.

CHAPTER 15

"Sharron, what are you doing here?" Mike asked flabbergasted.

Sharron didn't answer. Instead, she just pushed past him and walked into the living room. She looked around and saw the boys., "Get your stuff; I'm taking you home!"

Chris stared at her, "Mom, we've had this conversation. We're not going anywhere. I'm staying here, and Mikey doesn't want to go until school starts."

"I don't care what you want, and I don't care what you say. You're both coming home with me right now. I'll not have my children exposed to whatever is happening around this place," she said waving her hand around the room.

Mike stepped between them, "Sharron, there's nothing going on around here. The boys have been helping Kitty with her physical therapy and going to the pool every day. Then, when I get home we all eat and watch a little TV before bed. Just what do you think has been going on around here?"

"At this point, I don't care what's going on around here. I want my children out of here now! What kind of a parent are you, Mike? Exposing your kids to God only knows what? I can't tell you how many times my phone has rung with friends asking me what my son is doing hanging around a runaway heiress partying all hours of the night. Some of them have even insinuated he was having sex with this girl even though she's under eighteen. What am I supposed to tell my friends? What am I supposed to tell my parents?"

"You're not supposed to tell your parents anything, because there's nothing to tell them. Chris and Kitty went out one time. Unfortunately, it was just after the tabloids found out who she really was. In fact, we didn't know who she was until you called and told me."

"I don't care who she is or who you thought she was. I care about my children being exposed to you living with some underage little girl doing God only knows what for the last few months. You're sick! You repulse me and I'm not letting my children anywhere near you!"

"I'm sick? I'm not the one who walked out on our marriage. I'm not the one who started dating another guy while still married! You're the one who decided to do all that. You're the one who needs help. All I did was offer a young woman who had been badly beaten and left paralyzed a place to stay and heal. All I did was help a young woman rebuild her life. You're the one who's trying to make that act of kindness into some sort of evil, demented act of debauchery. Get you mind out of the gutter, Sharron! Open your eyes to the truth."

Sharron stood there stunned. Before she could say anything, Mike went on, "Before you condemn Kitty, why don't you stick around and meet her? She should be back soon. She went shopping with her friend Michelle D'Angelo, who just so happens to be a cop. And, while you're waiting, maybe you could calm down and relax a bit."

Sharron seemed to deflate before their eyes.

"Mom, sit down and I'll get you some iced tea." Chris offered.

"Alright, I'll wait and meet this girl, but then you're both coming back with me," Sharron announced as she walked over and sat on the couch.

"Are you going to tell me where you've been all afternoon, and what you've been up to, or will I have to guess?" Brian Madison asked his wife when she came through the door to their suite.

"I've been talking to Kitty and Mr. Hatfield," she announced as she sat on the couch and kicked off her shoes.

"Why?"

"I wanted to find out what's happened to our daughter since she ran away."

"And did you find out anything Mr. Long didn't tell us?"

"Yes. I found out our daughter has been brutally gang raped and beaten. I found out she's had her spleen and uterus removed and had back surgery to give her back the ability to walk. I also found out she'll have to use a cane for the rest of her life. And I found out her biggest fear is that you hate her."

"Hate her? I don't hate her."

"Brian, you saw our daughter for less than five seconds and succeeded in threatening to lock her in her room until she's twenty-one and have the man who was her guardian angel arrested for his good deeds. What did you expect her to think?"

Brian sighed, sitting down in the arm chair across from her. Rubbing his hand along his temples, he whispered, "Did I really say that?"

"Yes, you did."

"Well, I didn't mean it. I only meant I want her home with us where she's safe, and we can take care of her."

"Well, that's part of the problem. She's not a little child anymore. She wants her freedom but still wants to be able to come home, sort of like a safe harbor. It's just part of being sixteen."

Brian didn't say anything for a few seconds. Then he looked up and asked, "What do you think I should do?"

Carolyn smiled, "I'm glad you asked. I told Kitty we would like to take her and her friends out to celebrate the end of the rape case. I was thinking it would give us a chance to get to know her friends, and you can try to make up with your daughter."

"Okay, I'll make reservations at the best restaurant in town," he picked up the phone.

As he began to dial, Carolyn reached out and stopped him. "Let's let them make the arrangements. That way we'll learn more about how her life has been since she left home. Who knows, maybe we'll find out who our daughter really is. Maybe we'll find out what she likes and what she doesn't like. It'll be good for us and good for her too."

He put down the phone, "Okay, I'm not used to someone else being in charge, but I'll give it a try."

"Good," Carolyn picked up the phone and dialed Mike's number. Chris answered on the second ring. "Hello?"

"Hello, may I speak to Kitty Madison, please? This is her mother."

"Oh, hi Mrs. Madison. I'm Chris, Mike Hatfield's oldest son," Chris said. "Kitty went shopping with Michelle to look for a new outfit for the celebration tonight."

"Oh, that's why I'm calling. Her father and I thought we would like to let you guys decide where to go tonight. That is, if it's okay with everyone."

"That'd be great," Chris exclaimed. "We're thinking of going to Kirby's Steak House for dinner then there's a movie theater next door with a movie she wanted to see. I don't know what we're going to do after that."

"That sounds wonderful," Carolyn said. "What time would you like us there?"

"I guess around six or so would be good."

"Alright, we'll see you then." Carolyn hung up the phone with a satisfied smile on her face.

Kitty and Michelle got back to the apartment about an hour after Sharron arrived. When they walked through the door, they were greeted with stony silence. Kitty looked around and saw the reason right away. There was a woman she didn't know but instinctively assumed she was Mike's ex-wife.

Mike sprang up, "Kitty, Michelle, I'd like you to meet my wife... I mean ex-wife, Sharron. Sharron, this is Kitty Madison and Michelle D'Angelo."

Kitty put her shopping bag down and moved toward Sharron to greet her. She smiled and held out her hand, "It's nice to finally meet you, Mrs. Hatfield. Mike and the boys have told me so much about you."

Sharron took her hand but didn't smile. "I wish I could say the same."

Kitty's smile faltered. *What did she mean by that?*

Something of her thoughts must have shown on her face because Sharron continued, "I'm sorry. It's nice to finally meet you too. Unfortunately, Mike and the boys haven't told me very much about you. All they've said is that you're a nice girl who isn't sleeping with my husband."

Kitty's jaw dropped. "Sleeping with your husband? I don't think I understand. Whatever gave you the idea I was sleeping with your husband?"

"Well, let's think about that for a moment, shall we? You've been living alone with him in the same apartment for months. What would you think if you were me?"

"Mrs. Hatfield, in case no one told you, Kitty was brutally gang raped and beaten a couple of months ago. Until last month, she was paralyzed from the chest down. Not only was she not able to sleep with your husband. I'm sure after being raped, she had no desire to sleep with anyone, let alone a married man," Michelle's voice was hard a steel.

"Sharron, you're out of line!" Mike chided. "I've had enough of this. I've told you and the boys have told you that nobody has been sleeping with anybody. I think you'd better get your facts straight before you start accusing anyone of infidelity."

Kitty had tears in her eyes when she looked at Sharron. "How could you say such a thing? I'm a sixteen year old girl for God's sake Until I was attacked, I was a virgin. Since I was raped, I've been paralyzed and couldn't move. Mike has done nothing but care for me like a father would. I don't know what kind of girl you think I am, but I'm not the kind of girl who has an affair with a married man over twice my age."

Kitty turned and ran to her room. After slamming her door, she threw herself on her bed in tears. *How could that woman think such a thing?*

There was a knock on Kitty's door. "Go away!" she cried.

As she laid there crying, she heard the door open and close. She looked up and saw Michelle. "Kitty, I'm so sorry," she spoke softly. "Are you alright?"

Kitty sat up, "Yeah, I'll be okay. I guess I should have expected that. I suppose if I were in her shoes, I'd think the same thing. My father thinks it too."

"Nonsense," Michelle dismissed. "They just can't understand your relationship with Mike, that's all. Don't worry, they'll come around and everything will be okay. You'll see."

Mike stared at Sharron with a look of disgust that said plainly he couldn't believe what he'd just witnessed. He glanced at the boys and saw the same look on their faces. "Boys, why don't you take a walk. I want to speak to your mother alone." He stared hard at Sharron.

Chris and Mike got up and walked out the door without saying a word.

Mike walked over to the table, pulled out a chair, and sat looking at Sharron. "Sharron, what's going on?" he asked. "You're normally not a cruel person, and what I just witnessed was possibly the cruelest thing you've ever done. I know your upset, but I don't think it has anything to do with Kitty, me, or the boys." He looked her in the eyes, his gaze softening, "So, what's really wrong?"

Sharron immediately went on the defensive. "What makes you say that?" she asked. "I'm not upset about anything but you and that floozy."

"Sharron, we've known each other since junior high school. In all that time, don't you think I can tell when something isn't right? I know it's not Kitty or the boys because you weren't upset before we found out who she really was; so, why don't we stop playing games and you tell me what's the matter, maybe I can help."

Sharron looked like a balloon deflating as tears began to well up in her eyes. She looked down at her lap, "Mike, I don't know where to start." She looked up at him and continued, "When we moved in with my parents, I thought it was only going to be until I could get back on my feet. I found a job and met what I thought was a nice guy. Things were starting to come together. Then, after our divorce, Mom and Dad informed me they couldn't deal with me and the boys any longer. They said I needed to find a place for us to live. They were just too old to have teenagers around day in and day out. So I started looking for a place for us to live. That's when Kyle and I started getting serious. He was cute and nice and seemed to really like me for me. Boy, was I fooled."

Tears were now flowing down her cheeks as she continued. "At first, I thought he wanted to be with me, maybe even spend the rest of our lives together. He told me he wanted us to make a fresh start. He said he had a line on a new job out west and just needed some money to fly out there, start his job, and buy a house for us. He told me all we would need to start our new life together was ten thousand dollars." She laughed bitterly, "I guess there's no fool like an old fool. I borrowed and scraped together the money and gave it to him. I even drove him to the airport, kissed him goodbye, and watched him get on a plane for Phoenix. He promised to call when he arrived."

She wiped her cheeks with the back of her hand. "Well, as I'm sure you've figured out, my phone didn't ring. I tried calling his cell phone at least a dozen times. I left message after message, but he never called me back. I even tried calling the hotel he said he would be staying at. Only there wasn't any hotel by that name anywhere around Phoenix. Then I tried looking up the company he said he would be working for and found out it didn't exist either."

She paused and took a shuddering deep breath before she continued. "When I told Mom and Dad, they were heartbroken. They're the ones I borrowed most of the money from, you see. Dad told me he couldn't believe I was so stupid as to be swindled out of ten thousand dollars. He said they'd given me all the money they had in the world. Now, they didn't know how they were going to pay the extra bills that having me and the boys staying with them created. Dad said he was sorry, but we really needed to find some other place to live.

"I was shocked, to say the least. Where were we going to go? I decided to send the boys to visit you while I found a new place to live. It took me a while, but I finally found a little house on the outskirts of town I could afford. I signed the lease and just moved in when the other shoe fell, so to speak. I went to work the following week and was told the company was closing and moving overseas in two months. So, there I was... A forty year-old single mother of two with no job. I canceled the lease and lost my deposit, which was all the money I had left in the world. Homeless, no job, no money.

"That's when I saw the report about Chris and that girl on TV. I don't know why, but I just went off. I called you and then I called Chris and told him to come home." She laughed a bitter laugh again, "Home, what home? When he refused, I decided to come and get him and Mikey. I felt like I'd lost everything in my life. I'd be damned if I was going to lose my kids too. On the drive here, all I could think of was none of this would have happened if you hadn't let me down and lost your job. I know it was wrong, but I decided everything was your fault, and I needed to punish you and that girl."

Mike got up, walked over, and sat down beside her on the couch. He put his arm around her, "Why didn't you tell me earlier? I don't have much, but I would have sent you everything I could to help out. You know I still love you, I told you that on the phone."

She looked at his left ring finger and saw he still wore his wedding ring. "You still wear it?" she pointed to his hand. "Why?"

Mike blushed, "Because, I just couldn't bring myself to take it off. I know we're divorced, but in my mind, we're still married. I guess I'll always consider myself married to you."

She looked into his eyes, trying to find the lie in what he said. When she couldn't, she buried her face in his chest and broke down sobbing.

CHAPTER 16

They sat there on the couch for the longest time. Sharron felt the weight of all her worries flow out with her tears. Finally, she looked up, "Mike, I'm so sorry. I'm sorry I didn't believe in you after we lost everything. I'm sorry I divorced you for that swindler, and I'm sorry I accused you of having an affair with that poor girl. But, mostly, I'm sorry for the way I treated her. She didn't deserve that."

"It's nice of you to tell me, but don't you think you should tell her? I'm sure she's in the bedroom crying her eyes out, especially since her father said almost the same thing to her this morning."

Sharron looked up at him in astonishment, "Oh, my God! It's one thing for me to say that, but her own father told her that?"

"Yeah but I don't think he meant it either."

Sharron got up, "I'd better tell her how I really feel then." She walked to the bedroom door and knocked lightly.

A voice inside the room said, "Come in."

When Sharron came through the door, she saw Michelle sitting on the bed holding a sobbing Kitty. When she looked at the fragile young girl racked with pain she couldn't believe she'd been so cruel. "Excuse me, Miss Madison, I was wondering if I could talk to you for a moment," she asked hesitantly.

Kitty looked up with red swollen eyes. She didn't say anything, just stared at her.

Sharron took a step and closed the door. "I'm so sorry about what I said earlier. You didn't deserve any of it, and I know none of it's true. I was hurt and angry... And I took it out on you." She took another step inside the room, "I know there's nothing sexual between you and Mike. I know Mike's only been helping you. He's really a good man, and I guess I was jealous of your relationship. I really shouldn't have been. I should have seen it was more like a father-daughter relationship than anything else. You see, I once had a wonderful relationship with him too, but I threw it away on some pretty words and false promises. I'm so sorry."

When Sharron started talking, Kitty didn't want to hear anything she had to say, but then she found herself listening. As she looked at her, Kitty saw her eyes were red and puffy too. Sharron had obviously been crying she realized. "False promises?" she asked when Sharron finished talking.

Sharron took another step into the room, "Yeah, I was a stupid old woman who let a younger man take me for everything I had, promising me a wonderful life together he never intended to provide."

Michelle gently extracted herself from the bed and got up. "I'll leave you two alone so you can get better acquainted." She walked to the door. As she opened it, she looked back and saw Sharron sitting on the bed beside Kitty, telling her story. *Things will work out*, she thought.

When Sharron closed the door to the bedroom, Mike got up and walked to the kitchen. He opened a cabinet, took out the bourbon and poured himself a tall one. As he was sitting down, Chris and Mikey came back into the apartment. When they looked around and didn't see Sharron, Chris asked, "Where'd Mom go?"

Mike took a long sip of his drink, "She's in the bedroom apologizing to Kitty."

Just then Michelle came out and sat down next to Mike on the couch. As the boys each took seats, Mike asked, "How's Kitty? Has she calmed down?"

Michelle didn't answer right away. Instead, she asked, "Is there any more of that? I could sure use one."

Chris jumped up, "I'll make you one."

She smiled. "Thanks Chris, can you make it like your dad's?" Then she looked at Mike. "Well, at first she was pretty upset. I couldn't get her to say anything, she just sat there crying. Finally, she told me what her father said and a few other things. The poor girl was beside herself when your wife came in and apologized."

Chris handed her the drink, and she took a long pull on it. Sighing, she continued, "When I left, they were both sitting on the bed. Your ex was telling her why she said those mean things. I was surprised Kitty listened.

I know if it had been me, I would have thrown her out on her ear. But she didn't. I think everything will work out."

Kitty and Sharron spent the next hour closeted in Kitty's bedroom, each telling the other about their ordeal. In the end, they stepped out of the room as friends. When the door opened, Mike saw the two women smiling, looking as if they were the best of friends. He breathed a sigh of relief.

As they strode into the living area, Sharron asked, "Chris didn't I hear you tell the Madison's to be here around six?" When he nodded, she continued, "Well, don't you think you should be getting ready?"

The apartment became busy as the guys took turns in the bathroom, getting ready. The women used Kitty's room to do the same thing. As the last one finished showering, shaving, dressing or putting on makeup, the doorbell rang. To Kitty it seemed every face turned toward her. When she hesitated, Mikey jumped up from the couch, "I'll get it."

When he opened the door, he saw the Madison's standing there. He stepped back, "Come in."

Carolyn smiled and thanked him. She looked around and saw Kitty standing near the counter and smiled at her. Kitty smiled back. She walked over and gave Kitty a hug, leaving Brian standing by the door. He looked around uncomfortably, seeing less than friendly faces watching him. *Time to eat some crow,* he thought.

He cleared his throat. "I think before we go anywhere, I owe everyone an apology. I was out of line with almost everything I said this morning. There really is no excuse for my actions, I can only beg for your forgiveness."

Mike stepped over and offered him his hand, "Mr. Madison, I don't blame you for what you thought. If I had a daughter, I might have said the same thing."

They shook hands as Brian said, "Please, call me Brian. I appreciate your understanding of my motives, even if my actions were unforgivable."

There was an awkward silence, and Sharron stepped in to fill it. She got up and walked over to Brian. "It's nice to meet you Brian. I'm Sharron, Mike's wife... I mean ex-wife." She offered him her hand, and he shook it. She continued with the introductions, "And these are our sons, Christopher," Chris came over and shook Brian's hand. "And Michael Junior, we just call him Mikey." Mikey came over and shook Brian's hand too. "And this is Michelle D'Angelo. She's a police officer and friend of Mike's and Kitty's."

Michelle smiled and briefly waved from across the room.

Sharron went on, "Can I offer you a drink? Mike only has bourbon, but knowing my boys, there should be some Coke around here I can mix with it, if you'd like."

Brian moved further into the room. "That'd be great, Mrs. Hatfield."

As she walked into the kitchen area she stated, "Oh, just call me Sharron." Then she looked at Carolyn, "Can I fix you a drink too, Mrs. Madison?"

"It's Carolyn, and yes, I'd love one. But aren't we supposed to be leaving for the restaurant soon? Don't we have reservations for six o'clock?"

Chris spoke up, "Kirby's doesn't take reservations so there's no hurry." Then, looking at his mother, he said, "And I don't think there's any Coke in the fridge, but Mikey and I can run over to the pool and get a couple of cans from the vending machine if you want."

"That's an excellent idea," his mother replied. "I'll give you a couple of dollars, hang on."

"It's okay, Mom. I've got it," he replied and both boys were out the door in a flash.

Throughout their conversation, Brian was looking at his daughter. She was a stranger to him. *When did she grow up,* he wondered? *What happened to the little girl he used to tuck into bed at night?* When he looked at her now, he saw a beautiful young woman standing by his wife. *How did he miss her growing up?*

Kitty was looking at him. Through all the introductions and the ensuing conversations, she just stared at him. He could see the insecurity in her eyes. He could see the hurt there too. *Was that from what he had done and said, or from everything she'd been through?* He didn't know and he wasn't sure he wanted to know. If that insecurity was his fault he didn't think he could live with himself.

She watched him as he made his apologies. Kitty could see it cost him to admit he was wrong and made a fool of himself. As he shook everyone's hands, she could see the self-confident man she'd always known showing through. But when he looked at her, self-doubt was evident in his eyes. When Sharron broke the tension by beginning the introductions, Kitty saw the relief in his eyes. Still, he hadn't said anything to her. He'd barely looked at her, that is until this very moment.

When their eyes met, each saw confusion in the other's gaze. She tensed as her father began walking toward her. He stood before her and looked into her eyes. "Kitten," he whispered, "I'm so very sorry for all the mean, hateful things I said. Can you ever forgive me? Can we start again?"

She fell into his warm embrace and felt what she had missed for so long. This was the father she'd always wanted, but until now didn't realize she had him all along. Father, the one man who could make everything right. As they stood there hugging each other, both with tears in their eyes, the world seemed to melt away.

Kitty looked up into her father's eyes and saw tears softly falling. She whispered, "Daddy, I'm so sorry for hurting you and Mom. I don't know what I was thinking... And I had no idea things would turn out so badly. I guess I just wanted to grow up as fast as I could. I'm sorry."

They broke apart when Chris and Mikey came back in with the Cokes. Carolyn discretely handed both of them a tissue to wipe their eyes as Sharron finished mixing their drinks.

CHAPTER 17

After the drinks, they were ready to go to the restaurant. As they were preparing to walk out the door, Michelle asked, "How many cars are we taking? My car is a two-seater, so I can only take one other person."

Carolyn smiled. "We can take our car. There's plenty of room."

Michelle didn't understand until they walked out of the building's front door and saw the longest limousine she had ever seen. Chris and Mikey were fascinated. The two boys ran ahead and ogled the car while the others followed at a more leisurely pace.

It took only a few minutes to get to the restaurant and soon everyone was seated at a large round table. Once everyone ordered, Brian turned to Mike, "Carolyn tells me you work for Brewster and Simmons Investments. What do you think of the company?"

"I like it. The people are friendly, and the supervisors seem to really care about both the employees and the clients. That's a big change from my last employer."

"That's what we thought too," Brian said. "And, if you'll excuse me using Victor Kiam's old line, *we liked it so much we bought the company*."

They both laughed.

Carolyn was talking to Sharron, "You have a wonderful family. I think your boys are the nicest young people I've met in a long time. Your ex-husband is a saint. What he did for Kitty is amazing, especially since she was a complete stranger. When we first learned Kitty was living with a thirty-nine-year-old man, all sorts of things went through our minds. But, after talking to Kitty and your husband, we realized our fears were completely unfounded. Tell me, has Mike always been this kind to strangers, or is this something new?"

Sharron thought about her question for a moment. "Well, he's always been a kind, caring person. I can't tell you how many times I've seen him give homeless people money and food or how many stray animals he's brought home over the years. But Kitty's the first person he's ever brought home."

They both laughed.

"Well, I'm glad he did. I shudder to think what would have happened to her if he hadn't taken her in."

"Wouldn't she have just come home?"

"No, I don't think so. You see she and her father had a big fight the night she left. I don't think she would have come home under any circumstances." She was silent for a second, then added, "They love each other very much, but they're like fire and ice. They just can't get along. It's been that way since Kitty reached puberty. It's sad really."

"So, what do you think is going to happen now?"

Carolyn replied, "I don't know. I don't think she'll come home willingly, but I don't think she should stay with Mike much longer either. Once it gets out that she's living with him, there'll be photographers camped on their doorstep day and night, looking for anything unseemly. You know how they are. They'll make something up if they can't find anything."

Sharron agreed, "Just the fact they're living together would probably be enough for most tabloids."

Michelle was eavesdropping on their conversation and had a thought. "Excuse me, but I think I might have a solution to the problem."

Kitty and the boys were talking about the movie they were going to see after dinner. Chris was picking on her, "I can't believe a sixteen-year-old girl like you wants to go to a kid movie. I thought you wanted to see that chick flick that just came out."

"I do, but I want to see the new animated movie more." She winked, "Besides, it's not a chick flick, it's a date movie. I don't want to see it with my parents."

Chris blushed, "Well, maybe you and I should go see it without the grownups."

Kitty smiled, "Yeah, maybe we should."

After dinner was over, they walked next door to the theater and watched the movie. On the way out, both Chris and Mikey teased Kitty by imitating characters in the movie. Once outside the theater, the group stopped and talked about what they were going to do next.

Michelle suggested, ""I know this place that's not too far from here. It's an old style arcade, like you'd see at the beach. They've got pinball, skeet ball and all kinds of games and other things we can do. There's even dancing if you want to do that. And the best part is," she added with a grin, "They serve beer and wine to adults too."

Carolyn was feeling adventurous. Before anyone else could answer, she smiled and rubbed her hands together. "Oh, that sounds like fun. You know, when I was a girl, I was pretty good at pinball."

They all agreed and piled back into the limousine. Within a few minutes the car stopped at an open front building with a huge old fashioned flashing sign above the doors that read, "Aladdin's Cave of Many Wonders Arcade." When they got out of the car, they looked around in awe.

"This reminds me of when we took the kids to the beach, remember Mike," Sharron said. Then she turned to Michelle and asked, "This place is wonderful, how did you ever find it?"

Michelle smiled, "I was on patrol in the neighborhood and got a call here for a petty theft. After my shift was over, I came back and checked it out. It reminded me of the beach too. I love this place."

For the next three hours they all had a great time playing the arcade games and even dancing to the music. Although Mike, Sharron, Brian, and Carolyn played a few games, they spent most of their time listening to the music and sipping wine. Michelle stayed with the young people for about half the time, but spent the last hour or so with the older couples. Chris talked Kitty into a dance. Soon everyone was taking their turn dancing to the Classic Rock from the 50's and 60's.

As she watched Kitty dancing with Chris, Carolyn smiled to herself. She was glad to see Kitty was interested in the boy. After all her daughter had been through, it would have been understandable if she never wanted anything to do with boys ever again. The only thing that made her uncomfortable was that she was living in the same apartment as this boy.

Finally, everyone was tired and ready to go home. It was after midnight when they stepped out of the club. The limousine was parked two blocks away. Brian pulled out his cell phone to call the driver. The limo had just stopped at the traffic light when their attention was drawn away.

The sound of police sirens caused the group to look around. They saw a dark sports car speed around the corner, police cars following in its wake. As it rounded the corner, the rear wheels fishtailed, and the vehicle began spinning. Mike had only seconds to act. He pushed Sharron and Michelle back toward the front of the arcade and yelled to the others to get out of the way. He was moving back too when the right fender of the sports car slammed into him from behind, sending in spiraling into the air before it smashed into the light pole.

Michelle and the others watched in horror as the black sports car slammed into Mike. As if in slow motion, they watched his body fly into the air, flipping over and over. When he slammed down hard, his body smashed into the windshield of the car and roll off. Once the car came to a stop. Michelle ran over to it.

Following her training, Michelle did several things at once. As she was running to the car, she saw Mike was seriously hurt. She knew she wasn't trained to do anything for him but keep him still until the EMT's arrived. Reaching the driver's side window, she saw the driver was also injured. Quickly assessing him, she realized although he was bleeding for a thousand little cuts from the shattered windshield glass, the airbag seemed to have prevent further damage. He didn't appear to be in immediate danger. Knowing he had been running from the police, there was a chance once he recovered from his temporary stupor, he could panic and try to drive away. Michelle quickly opened the door and put the gearshift in 'Park' while pulling out the keys from the ignition.

Once done, she turned her attention back to Mike. She could see his chest rising, but she could also see blood trickling from his mouth, nose, and ears. She's seen symptoms like that before and knew he was in critical condition.

Sharron watched in horror as Mike was mowed down by the sports car. Her first instinct was to run to him, but Michelle stopped her. Instead, she grabbed onto Mikey and Chris, keeping them from running to their father. She held Mikey tightly as she watched the drama unfold.

Chris screamed out as his father flew into the air and crashed down on the car. As he stepped toward the scene, both his mother and Kitty barred his progress. At first he tried to push past the two women but finally stopped struggling. Instead, he held Kitty and watched Michelle tend to his father, tears streaming down his cheeks.

Carolyn and Brian watched in horror as Mike was pummeled by the speeding car. They couldn't tear their eyes away as they watched Mike flip over and over and crash back onto the car. Brian instinctively pulled out his cell phone and dialed 9-1-1. But, he needn't have bothered, as three police cars, sirens blaring, screeched to a stop in front of them.

The cops raced out of their cars, running to the accident scene. One of them recognized Michelle. They worked together to try to help Mike while some of the other officers saw to the driver of the car. One look at Mike's crumpled body, and they decided not to move him, waiting for the ambulances to arrive.

The ambulance crews carefully placed Mike's broken body onto a backboard and then onto the gurney. Sharron pulled away from Mikey and ran to her ex-husband's side. They loaded him into the back of the ambulance, and Sharron followed. Within seconds the ambulance was on its way to the nearest hospital.

When Sharron ran to Mike's side, Carolyn moved over to Mikey. She held him as they watched his mother and father get into the ambulance and drive away. As the ambulance screamed into the night, Mikey buried his face in Carolyn's shoulder. She looked around and saw tears in everyone's eyes.

As soon as Brian hung up from the 9-1-1 dispatcher, he called the chauffeur and told him to get as close as he could to them and wait. After the ambulance drove away from the scene, Brian walked over to Michelle and called, "I'll take the others and go to the hospital. I'll send the car back for you, if you want."

Busy with the accident scene, Michelle shook her head. She told Brian she would get one of the other officers to bring her to the hospital when they finished processing the scene. He nodded and went over to gather up the others. Gently, he guided them to the limousine, and they left for the hospital.

The man had been following the Madisons all evening, filming them going in and coming out of the restaurant, movie theater, and arcade. As he saw the Madison party come out of the arcade he raised his camera and began filming. When he heard the police sirens coming toward them, he swung around just in time to catch the sports car losing control and slamming into Mike. *This was good stuff,* he thought! He continued to film the event as the police tended to Mike and the driver of the car. He kept filming as the ambulance crew loaded Mike into the ambulance and took off for the hospital. When the Madison party got into their limousine, he ran, jumped into his car, and followed. While he was chasing the limousine, he called his contact at the TV station.

Through the corner of his eye, Mike saw the sports car coming at him. He knew he was going to get hit, he just hoped it didn't hurt too much. For a split second the pain was overwhelming, and then it was gone.

The next moment, Mike was lying on his back, the sun shining through his closed eyelids and a cool breeze blew across his face. He figured he must be dead, because if he wasn't dead, he knew he should be in considerable pain. Funny, he felt fine. No pain. Surprisingly, he felt no fear or anxiety either. He wanted to just lie there enjoying the warm sun and soft breezes forever.

He heard a familiar voice. "Michael," the voice began. "Come, walk with me."

Mike shaded his eyes and looked up. He saw the familiar man in the white robe standing near his feet. Mike scrambled up and looked into the man's calm, smiling face. The man held out his arm and placed it around Mike's shoulder as they began walking.

"You've done well, Michael," the man said. "I'm proud of you."

"What have I done?"

"Do you remember when you were here last time, and I said you still had work to do?"

 Mike thought back. As the memory returned, he answered, "Yes, I remember."

"Did you ever wonder what that work was?"

Slowly Mike said, "Yeah, I wondered. In fact, I still wonder what it was or even if I did it."

The man smiled, "When I sent you back, I gave you a job to do, and you did it. You showed a young girl what love and compassion really are. You didn't ask her for anything. You just wanted to help. That was a lesson she needed to learn for the future I have planned for her. You also reminded her parents of the value of the gift I gave them sixteen years ago. And, perhaps just as importantly, you showed your own family what really matters. Not money, not possessions, but friends and family. Michael, you've done the job I wanted you to do better than I could have hoped."

Mike thought about what the man said. *Had he really done all that just by helping Kitty? Did he really do so much?* The idea he had done all that was mind-boggling.

The man went on, "It's amazing what one simple act of kindness and love can accomplish, isn't it? You know Kitty, her family, and your family aren't the only ones who learned something. You did too."

Mike was amazed. He looked at the man next to him, "What did I learn?"

The man chuckled, "You, my friend, learned unselfishness and the power of love. As you continued to care for Kitty, you changed. You began showing love and compassion to others too. Your co-workers, your clients, your family, strangers, everyone you came into contact with. Each person you encountered came away feeling like you really cared about them and their problems. You brought the light of love into their lives and taught them how to share."

Mike was silent as they walked, deep in thought. There was a lot to think about. "I guess I did some good, didn't I?"

"Amazing isn't it? And to think you once wanted to throw all that away. Think of the loss your earlier selfish decision would have caused."

They stopped at the edge of a pool. The man looked at Mike, "And now Michael, you have a decision to make. Will you go back, or will you stay?"

CHAPTER 18

For a moment Mike wasn't sure he heard right. "The last time I was here, you said I'd be staying the next time I came back, didn't you?"

"No. What I said was, the next time you come back you may stay. May and must are two very different things. No, Michael, I'm giving you the choice. You can stay here with your mother, father, and all the other people you have loved who've crossed over, or you can go back to your children, other family, and friends. The choice is yours."

Mike looked down into the sparkling waters of the pool that lay before them. Suddenly, he could see down into an operating room at the hospital. In the vision, doctors and nurses were working feverishly on a man lying on the table. Then, the scene changed and Mike saw his family and friends in the waiting room. Sharron was holding Mikey as they both cried. Kitty was holding Chris. Both had a look of shock and fear on their faces. Brian and Carolyn sat together in silence holding hands.

The scene changed again to the police station where the driver of the sports car was being processed. Mike could see him and the arresting officer sitting at a table, the man taking a breath test, his face covered with bandages. He could see the waiting area of the police station and a woman with a small child waiting. Mike assumed the woman was the man's wife. He could see tears in her eyes and could see a little boy in her arms, a look of fear on his face.

Mike looked up, "So much pain. So much misery. Why?"

The robed man looked at him, "When Adam and Eve ate the fruit from the Tree of the Knowledge of Good and Evil, they received both knowledge and the free will to use it. From that time forward, mankind has used his knowledge and free will to bring many evils into the world. Evils that were never intended. The price of knowledge wasn't just exile from paradise. The price also included responsibility for one's actions. You see, Michael, every decision comes with a consequence. When that man decided to drink too much alcohol and run from the police, he didn't realize the price that would have to be paid for his decision.

"He and his family will pay a heavy price. You and your family will bear some of that burden too. But the decision of how much is yours. If you remain here, your friends and family will pay the price of grief and loss of a loved one, you.

"Kitty and her family will lose a good and caring friend. Your company will lose one of its best employees, and you will lose the joys and sorrows you would have experienced from this point forward. The man you saw in the police station will be charged with Vehicular Manslaughter and convicted. His family will suffer more pain and hardship if you stay than they would if you went back.

"If you go back, there will still be pain. Your family and friends will feel the pain of watching you struggle to recover. The man in the police station will still spend time in jail and he'll still have to live with the consequences of his actions. But, most of the pain and suffering will fall on your shoulders.

"You will struggle for months, trying to recover from your injuries. And, who knows, you may never really fully recover. But your struggles could bring encouragement and hope to others. Your helplessness may allow others to experience the joy of helping another. It may very well be that your pain and suffering will serve as an example to others who are learning to live and recover from serious injuries or illnesses. Perhaps, by going back, your struggles will bring your family together in a way they may never have achieved otherwise. And then, there's Kitty and her family. If you return, you may give them the opportunity to learn how to show their love by helping others.

"You see, Michael, your decision, as with all decisions, affects more than just you."

Mike stood staring at the pool, not really seeing anything. *What should he do?* His head told him one thing, but his heart told him another. He looked up into the man's face and saw only love and concern.

The man whispered, "I can't make this decision for you Michael. It's up to you."

Mike took a deep breath, "If I go back, will Sharron and I get back together? I don't think I could do it without her."

The man smiled. "Whether you two get back together or not, you're soul mates. You will always be in each other's hearts."

Mike laughed. "That doesn't help. Can't you be a little less vague?"

The man chuckled, "Normally no, but in this case I'll make an exception. Yes. You and Sharron will get back together. She will dedicate herself, at least in the short term, to your recuperation. You'll get remarried and live together for as long as you both live. Does that help you to make your decision?"

"Yes, it does," Mike replied. "It helps a lot." He paused and looked down at the pool again. The doctors and nurses were frantically working on the man. "Will I ever see you again?" Mike asked, still not looking at the man.

The man smiled again. "I will be with you always. Whenever you need me, you'll find me here." He tapped on Mike's chest, above his heart. "I have always been there, Michael. You just never looked before."

"We're losing him," one of the doctors yelled.

"I've lost the pulse!"

"Defibrillator, stat," yelled another doctor.

The machine was wheeled up next to the operating table. The doctor took the two paddles and held them out to a nurse. She spread gel on them and the doctor rubbed them together before placing them on the man's chest. "Clear!" he yelled. A second later the body jumped as the electricity jolted the heart.

"No change," called another voice.

"Again," the lead doctor called. He placed the paddles back on the chest and cried, "Clear!"

Again the body jumped as the electricity surged through it.

"That's it! I've got a pulse," yelled one of the doctors.

The lead doctor took a deep breath, "Okay people, let's finish up before we lose him again."

Six hours. It's been six hours since they took Mike into the operating room, and we haven't heard a word, Sharron thought. *Oh God, please don't take him, not now. Please give him back to us.* She looked at the others. They were all still there: Kitty and her parents, Michelle, and of course, the boys. Everyone looked lost in their own thoughts and feelings. Tension filled the room with an uncomfortable silence.

Suddenly, the doors at the end of the hall opened and a tired middle aged man in scrubs came walking toward them. Everyone looked up and watched him as he came nearer. One look at the man's face told Sharron it was bad news. As he neared the waiting area, she stood up. He announced, "He's alive. We stopped the internal bleeding as best we could, but he's not out of the woods yet. If he can survive the next twenty-four to thirty-six hours, he should be strong enough for us to go back in and repair some of his other injuries. But, right now, he's just not strong enough. I'm sorry, Mrs. Hatfield. I wish I had better news, but that's the best we could hope for given the circumstances."

Sharron couldn't speak. She just nodded.

The doctor patted her on the shoulder reassuringly, "He's fighting hard to stay alive, and we're fighting hard to keep him that way. I can't say for certain, but I believe he's got a sixty percent chance. That's better than most patients I've seen with these types of injuries." He smiled a weary smile. "Somebody up there must like him. He's being taken to Intensive Care right now. You should be able to visit him in a few minutes."

Sharron found her voice, "Thank you, Doctor."

The surgeon patted her shoulder again and walked away.

She turned to the others and gave them a watery smile. "I'm going to the Intensive Care Unit to see him. Why don't the rest of you go home and get some rest? If anything changes, I'll call you."

At first, the boys began to protest, but Sharron insisted.

Finally, Brian stood up, "Let's go get something to eat, go home, and rest for a while. We'll come back later in the afternoon, is that good?"

The boys finally agreed, and they all left as Sharron headed for the ICU.

When she entered the room, a group of nurses were hooking up monitors and IVs. After a few minutes, they finished and left. Sharron sat in a chair near the window and stared blankly at the monitors. Her eyes drifted to Mike's swollen and bruised face. She silently cursed herself for ever leaving him. Now she wondered if she would ever get him back.

As they were walking out to the limo, Carolyn asked Kitty where she was going to go. "I'm going to go back to the apartment, where else would I go?"

"Well," Carolyn started, "With Mike in the hospital and Sharron needing a place to sleep, don't you think you should give her your room? You could stay with us for a while. We're not going anywhere until we find out if Mike will make it or not. That way, you can reacclimate yourself to living with us again."

Kitty didn't say anything, but Carolyn could see in her face she didn't think much of the idea. "I'm not sure that'll work. The reason I ran away from home was because I couldn't live with you guys. I don't think anything has changed, do you?"

Carolyn frowned, "Kitty, after all you've been through, don't you think you've changed? And, considering all we've been through, maybe we've changed too. Why don't you give us a chance? Consider it a trial run."

In the end, she agreed. After dropping everyone else off at the apartment, Kitty packed a few belongs for the hotel trial run. Three days later, all three of them realized it wasn't going to work.

"Daddy," Kitty began, "I love you and Mom dearly. I never want to do anything to hurt either one of you again, but I don't think I can live with you."

Brian didn't like it, but deep in his heart, he knew it was true. Yet, he also knew she was still only sixteen. "I know Kitten, but you're too young to be off on your own."

Carolyn interjected, "Michelle was saying something about having an idea about Kitty's living arrangements, but she never got the chance to explain. Maybe I should call her and find out what she had in mind? Maybe there's a good solution we haven't seen yet."

Michelle spent as much time with the boys as she could. It was a couple of days later when she met up with the Madisons at the hospital. Carolyn took her aside, "Do you remember the night of the accident when Sharron and I were talking about Kitty's future?"

Michelle thought for a few seconds, "Yeah, I remember."

"Well, you said you had an idea but there was never time to elaborated on it before the accident. What was your idea?"

"Oh, that. Well, I was thinking, if Kitty didn't want to move back home again, she could move in with me. I've got plenty of room, and there's a private high school about two blocks away. I don't have a roommate, and it's kind of lonely rattling around by myself."

"Kitty isn't adjusting well to living with Brian and I at the hotel, and I think it's only going to get worse back at the house. Your idea sounds like the best solution I've heard. Maybe, after we leave the hospital today, we could come with you to see your place. Then, Kitty can see if she likes it. I'll have to talk to Brian though. He's not happy with her not living at home; he's kind of old fashioned. But living with a police officer might give him peace of mind."

Michelle nodded in agreement.

Mike remained in a coma for over a week. A steady stream of doctors and specialists examined him daily. He was taken back to the operating room three more times to repair something they hadn't found the first few times. Eventually, his injuries were finally all treated: bones set and wounds healing. Things were settling into a routine of waiting when it happened.

All of a sudden, Mike opened his eyes and moaned.

Sharron was at his side in an instant.

After he left the man in the robe, Mike felt as if he was floating in a dark pool. There was no feeling, no sound, and no light. You would think it would be kind of scary, but Mike found it quite peaceful. Slowly, over a period of days, he began coming out of the pool, as he thought of it.

From time to time he could hear people talking, and every now and then, he thought he could see the darkness growing lighter. He knew he was out of the pool when he was gripped with pain. It started slowly, almost imperceptibly, and began to build. As the pain increased, it began to spread. Just before he opened his eyes, Mike felt as if every square inch of his body had been bruised and battered. Without really meaning to or even realizing he did it, he let out a soft moan and opened his eyes.

The lights were low but to Mike it seemed as if spot lights were aimed directly at his eyes. He blinked, trying to clear the spots, when he felt someone take his hand. Even though it hurt, as everything did, it also felt reassuring. Then he heard the one voice he had wanted to hear since he came back. Sharron softly called his name, "Mike?"

She looked at his eyes, and they seemed unfocused. For a heartbeat she feared his eyes opened of their own accord but he wasn't really awake. When his eyes turned and focused on her face, she felt herself smile and let out a breath she didn't know she'd been holding. It was the first time she'd smiled since the accident.

When the nurses saw Mike awake, they made Sharron leave while the doctor examined him. She used the time to call the others to tell them Mike was awake. After about a half an hour, she was allowed back into his room. She smiled as she walked back in, "How are you feeling?"

CHAPTER 19

The road to recovery was a long one with many bumps. There were times Mike wondered what he was thinking when he told the man in the white robe he wanted to come back. But, no matter what, Sharron was there by his side. The only time she left was when there was someone else visiting, usually one of the boys.

Through the haze of pain and medication, Mike noticed whenever he saw Chris, Kitty was usually there too. He was glad she had someone to rely on and hoped she wouldn't get hurt. He knew Chris would be good to her and wouldn't be the one to break her heart.

Brian and Carolyn visited a few times. One memorable time, Dr. Boyd was talking to Mike about his many broken bones and how they were healing. When Brian and Carolyn walked in, Brian said, "Oh, we're sorry. We didn't know you had someone with you."

As they turned to go, Mike called out, "Wait a minute, don't go. I'd like you to meet someone."

They turned around, and Mike said, "Doc, this is Brian and Carolyn Madison. They're Kitty's parents. Brian, Carolyn, this is Dr. Ronnie Boyd. He's the doctor who performed Kitty's back surgery so she could walk again."

As Ronnie stood up, Brian held out his hand, and Ronnie shook it. Carolyn gave him a giant hug. "Thank you so much for taking care of our little girl, Doctor. I can't tell you how much it means to us."

Ronnie returned the hug. "You're very welcome. Your daughter is a wonderful person, and I was only too glad to help." Then he added, "But I thought her last name was Benson, not Madison."

"Yes, well... she went by an alias after she ran away. It's interesting she chose that name. Benson was my maiden name."

"So, how's Mike doing," Brian asked.

Ronnie looked at Mike who nodded his permission. "Well, he's getting better. I figure he'll be back on his feet in a month or two."

The four of them talked for a while; then Brian and Carolyn thanked Ronnie again as he left. Soon after, Sharron came in and joined the conversation. Mike told her what Ronnie said, and, shortly after that, Brian and Carolyn left.

When they were alone, Mike decided to bring up a subject he'd been thinking about a lot lately. "Sharron, the school year will be starting soon. Have you and Mikey decided what you're going to do?"

Sharron hedged, "What do you mean?" She thought knew exactly what he meant, but she wanted to hear what he was thinking before she let him know the arrangements she'd already made.

"Well," he began nervously, "If Mike's going to go to school at your parents' house, you'll need to get back there pretty soon." He stopped. He didn't want to pressure her into staying, although he was hoping they would.

Sharron slowly stated, "He doesn't really want to go back there, and I really don't have a reason to go back either. But still, that's an option I guess." After a moment she added, "I don't know, maybe I'll find a place around here to live so he can go to school here. You're not going to be in the hospital forever, and when you get out, you'll probably need someone to take care of you until you get back on your feet. I thought... Maybe I could help out for a while... Just until you get back on your feet, that is."

Mike smiled. He couldn't help himself. "Well, my apartment's going to be a little crowded, but I guess we'll manage."

Time to let the cat out of the bag, she thought.

"Oh, you don't live in that little apartment anymore," Sharron said casually, "We have a nice three bedroom apartment in the same building as Michelle."

Mike's mouth dropped open in shock. He didn't know what to say.

Sharron laughed at the look on his face. "Sorry, but when I explained to the landlord about your accident and inability to work, he agreed to let you out of the lease. The Madisons insisted on helping with the deposit and first couple of months of rent for a new apartment. Mikey's already registered at the same school Kitty's going to, and Chris is registered at the community college."

Mike continued to look at her incredulously.

"And Carolyn helped me get a job with the same company you work at, in the accounting department. I start as soon as they let you out of here, so I can help with bills."

Mike grinned, "So, does that mean we're a family again?"

Sharron dropped her eyes shyly, "Only if you want to be. I left you remember? And, because I'm the one who left, I have no right to assume I can come back into your life."

"Do you want to come back?" Mike asked.

Sharron looked up, "Only if you want me to."

As she looked into his eyes, Mike replied, "I think I told you once that you were the only woman I ever loved. It was true then and it's still true today. Of course I want you back! I never wanted you to leave."

Sharron stood and walked over to the bed. She leaned over to hug him. "Mike, I love you. You're the only man I ever truly loved. I'm so sorry. If you're willing to forgive me, I really want to be Mrs. Michael Hatfield again."

Mike pulled her into a one-handed embrace, "I'd like that very much."

Two weeks later, Mike got out of the hospital. Arrangements were made for a nurse and a physical therapist to come to their apartment three times a week to help Mike with his recovery. At first, he was in a wheelchair, but before long, he was hobbling around on crutches. Finally, Mike was using a cane and began to get bored sitting around the house. It was time to go back to work.

The boys began classes on the same Monday Mike went back to work. After saying goodbye to the boys, Sharron and Mike went to work together. As he walked into the office, his coworkers applauded and welcomed him back. It was a good feeling to know he had been missed.

Mike and Sharron worked on plans for their wedding for months. Since they had eloped the first time, Sharron wanted a church wedding this time. It took a lot of explaining before the priest understood their unique situation and could persuade the Archdiocese to approve their wedding, but finally, everything was ready for the big day.

Mike asked Brian to be his Best Man and Brian was shocked but honored. He, of course agreed. Sharron asked Carolyn to be her Matron of Honor and she too agreed. The boys were ushers, and Kitty and Michelle were the bride's maids.

When the big day came, the church was filled with friends, family and coworkers. Mike and the boys were standing at the altar when the organist began playing "*Here Comes the Bride.*" They turned as one and saw Michelle and Kitty walking down the aisle in their autumn gold dresses.

Once they were about half way down the aisle, Sharron and her father appeared in the doorway. Mike beamed as he saw his bride being escorted down the aisle. She was as beautiful as the first time they wed. Wearing a sophisticated ivory wedding dress, she still took his breath away. The wedding and reception looked right out of a fairy tale. He couldn't believe his good fortune. After a short honeymoon in the Caribbean, Mike and Sharron went back to work and fell into the familiar routine of day-to-day living.

Mike often reflected on his time on the other side and his miraculous return to life, twice. He thought he finally understood the beauty of struggle. Every day was an opportunity to show love and kindness. From experience, Mike knew one small act of random kindness could changed the world. After all, it had changed his world and Kitty's.

He looked up and winked, knowing the man in the robe could see him.

Life was good!

Thank you for reading, Kindness of a Stranger.

Scott A. Ferguson, Sr. has new release coming 2024:

Marcus Cooper

www.ingramcontent.com/pod-product-compliance
Lightning Source LLC
Chambersburg PA
CBHW030837200726
48285CB00007B/2466